Revenge

When buffalo hunter O'Brien is wrongly accused of rustling by ranch hands and has to kill the rancher's son to defend himself from hanging, he thought his life had already taken a bad turn. However, within a day's ride from that violent scene, he happens upon Sarah Carter.

Together they follow the dangerous road to Fort Revenge, where Sarah is due to wed Jake Latimer. It becomes clear that Latimer is not the man for Sarah, but can O'Brien save Sarah as well as dealing with his own troubles from the past. . . .

Fort Revenge

Ralph Hayes

A Black Horse Western

ROBERT HALE · LONDON

© Ralph Hayes 2011
First published in Great Britain 2011

ISBN 978-0-7090-9226-1

Robert Hale Limited
Clerkenwell House
Clerkenwell Green
London EC1R 0HT

www.halebooks.com

Typeset by
Derek Doyle & Associates, Shaw Heath
Printed and bound in Great Britain by
CPI Antony Rowe, Chippenham and Eastbourne

CHAPTER ONE

It was open, arid plain where the wagon stopped. As far as the eye could see, there was only high prairie grass, granjeno, and jumping cholla. They had just entered Indian Territory, and it was known that several renegade bands of Pawnee and Mescalero had caused travelers trouble in that area recently, so the two drivers had been watchful all through the long day's ride. The men climbed down from the freight-loaded conestoga and picketed the team where it stood, and the short, middle-aged one walked around back to check on their lone passenger.

Sarah Carter sat uncomfortably on her large shipping trunk back there, looking dusty, tired, and disconsolate. It seemed a lifetime ago when she had begun this difficult pilgrimage.

'We're going to stop here for a rest, ma'am,' the fellow called Jervis told her as he released the tailgate. 'Best you get down and stretch your legs.'

She was staring out over the desolate landscape. 'Is this the kind of country I'll be going to at Fort Revenge?' she asked wearily. Just past her thirtieth birthday, she was dark-haired and fairly pretty, but with fine lines already around her green eyes.

5

'Oh, no, ma'am. This here is a mite more likable than where you're headed.'

Sarah shot a dour look his way as the other driver, a man called Guthrie, returned from watering the horses. He was rough-looking, with a scraggly beard, but he and Jervis had treated Sarah like a lady. 'There's a little creek about thirty yards down that slope, ma'am. You might want to freshen up before we set out again.'

Sarah nodded. 'Thanks, Mr Guthrie. I might just do that.'

She had paid her fare to the Kansas and Missouri Freight Company over a week ago, because no stage company offered service in this direction. Jervis helped her off the wagon, and she took a towel and headed down to the small stream nearby. And as she walked, she remembered the beginnings of all this. It had been a cold April day in Boston when she read the item in the local newpaper:

YOUNG WOMEN WANTED TO SETTLE IN THE WEST.

There had been a reference to a travel agent, in the Haymarket Square area. Long ago bored with her job at the Boston City library, and with her life in general after two failed romances, Sarah had all but given up on making a marriage and a family. But the advertisement had piqued her curiosity, and the very next day she visited the agency, and listened to enthralling stories of the Great West and the lonely but deserving men out there who longed for a female companion to make a real home for them on the frontier.

Sarah had arrived at the creek now, and saw that the tall rushes and high grass afforded her complete privacy from the wagon. The rushing, clear water looked cool and inviting and she was pleased with this unexpected luxury. She removed a frilly blouse and dipped part of the towel into the water, still remembering those days in Boston. Her interview at the agency had ended with the agent proffering her the name of a rather young farmer type named Jacob Latimer, who lived in the Oklahoma Territory in a small town called Fort Revenge, after a closed-down cavalry fort nearby. Latimer had been described to her as an affable, industrious fellow who would make her a fine husband, and a local magistrate would join them in holy matrimony immediately upon her arrival. Sarah impetuously succumbed to this sales pitch, and a few days later, abandoning her job and few friends, she headed west on a smoke-belching train to fulfill her covenant to become a mail-order bride. Now, it seemed like that had happened in another century, and in an entirely different universe.

Kneeling at the creek's edge, she splashed water on her face and arms, and enjoyed its soothing touch; it felt wonderful after this last long, hot ride.

Up at the wagon, things weren't as tranquil. Guthrie had looked up from adjusting a harness buckle when he squinted down hard. A hundred yards away, a small band of rogue Pawnee, off their reservation, were staring down at them from a low hill. They were mounted and wearing war paint. There were five riders in all.

'Jervis,' Guthrie said quietly. 'Looks like we got company.'

Gray-haired Jervis looked up startled, and mumbled a profanity under his breath. Both men wore sidearms, but their rifles were on the wagon.

'It's a war party,' Guthrie said, his heart pounding.

'I'm going for the long guns,' Jervis said tersely. 'Stay put.'

But their time was too short. With a loud war-whoop, the Pawnee were suddenly thundering down on them, firing arrows as they came. Jervis managed to get up on to the seat of the wagon and was reaching for a rifle when the first arrow struck him violently in the side. Guthrie now ran in a panic for Jervis's dropped rifle, but the Indians were all around the wagon now, kicking up dust, and in just seconds he had two arrows in him, in his back and left thigh.

Down at the creek, Sarah had turned in terror at the sound of the Indians' yelling, and now grabbed her blouse and crouched low in the bullrushes, out of sight of the mêlée at the wagon. She heard Guthrie scream amid the clamor of the Pawnee, and then things went quiet as the attackers cut the horses loose. One brave pried Sarah's trunk open and threw some clothing around but didn't understand the significance of the find, thinking it was just freight. They soon rode off with their booty, never seeing Sarah down at the stream.

Sarah waited almost an hour after all the noise had subsided before she warily emerged from cover and returned to the wagon. She gasped when she saw what had happened. Guthrie and Jervis lay sprawled on the ground, their bodies bristling with arrows. She turned away and was sick on the ground beside the wagon. When she was able, she took a closer look at the mess. The horses were gone, their harness trappings lying in the dirt. The wagon was intact, but anything of value had been stolen, including some of Sarah's clothing. They had taken the shoes off the men's feet, and scalped them both.

After a long moment staring in disbelief at the carnage that surrounded her, Sarah slumped down against a big spoked wheel and began to quietly sob.

A few hours later, and fifty miles to the north, the sun was lowering in the western sky where two men were encamped near a small stand of cottonwoods. The men were aging buffalo hunters in a country where the buffalo were very nearly gone, and their livelihood had disappeared with the great herds. Now they were forced to trap beaver and ermine for a living, and even that occupation was becoming more difficult.

One of the two men had been hunting in the West for over two decades, and his name was well known by others of his kind. He had emigrated there from the hills of Tennessee as a very young man, when his family had been taken down by the dyphtheria. Buffalo men knew him simply as O'Brien, and he never acknowledged having been given any other. He had worked for a big hide company for a while, but then went out on his own to hunt the 'shaggies'. There had been temporary partnering with some of the greats like Shanghai Smith and Jim Elder, but mostly he had hunted alone. It was Elder who had said O'Brien could hit a buffalo between the eyes at five hundred yards in a stiff crosswind with his Sharps .500 rifle. He was an honorary brave of three Indian tribes in the Great Plains, and a story spread among them that he had emerged full-grown from a bear cave near Ogallala just a few dozen moons ago.

Now, though, at well over forty and aging with every trail he rode, those old free-and-easy days on the buffalo hunt were a time of the distant past.

On that rather cold, moonless night in March, he hunkered over a low fire with another temporary partner who was called Curly Davis. Davis had asked to ride south with O'Brien into Oklahoma Territory, to find better trapping grounds there. They now sat hunkered over their fire, O'Brien poking pensively at the glowing embers as Davis grumbled about the vagaries of life on the trail. Earlier they had broiled slabs of salt pork on green sticks and put them down with a few stale corn dodgers, and were now boiling coffee in a used tomato tin. They had saved the grease from the salt pork to make biscuits at the next camp, and to spread on their boots and saddlery.

'I'm not sure how much longer I can do this,' Davis was saying, continuing his ramblings about the life he had led. 'A man can only last through so many miles of sore butts, riding kinks, and sour stomachs from trail grub.'

O'Brien poked at the fire, and bright, fiery embers exploded into the growing darkness. 'You picked it,' he offered. 'It don't pick you.'

'Do you ever get lonesome?' Davis persisted, looking over at him. 'I mean, saggy-eyed, dead-out lonesome? Where you'd trade the horse you're riding on for just a few words with another human being?'

O'Brien turned and regarded him narrowly. He now had some gray in his hair, but was still hard-bellied, wide-shouldered, and athletic-looking. He wore rawhides and a full beard, and had long, wild-looking hair under his trail-colored Stetson. This was what he didn't like about riding with a partner. They usually tried to talk you to death.

'Maybe you need a good laxative, Davis,' he finally replied sourly.

'I had this woman, a few years back in Kansas. Ugly as sin, but she could make a beef stew that made you think you'd died and gone to heaven. You ever have yourself a woman? I mean, to live with?'

O'Brien wrapped his hand in a piece of burlap, retrieved the tomato can from the fire, and poured the chicory coffee into their two cups. He handed one to Davis. 'Can't say I have,' he said. He had never found any time to meet a woman, except on a casual basis. He had never really gotten past the eternal fight for survival – against the plains, and

10

against other men. He sipped his coffee.

Davis sighed. 'I hope you're right about good trapping down south of here. I ain't never heard nothing good about the Territory. You'd think the redskins would have cleaned out all the decent game thereabouts. Say, did I ever tell you about the time I rode six hundred miles on word of a big herd of shaggies, only to find the area littered white with bones and rotten meat? Vultures was so thick over them remains you could shoot into the air without aiming and hit one.'

O'Brien shook his head. They were squatting on dry logs, their horses picketed to the stand of cottonwoods a short distance away. 'A few years back there was a cowpoke out by hisself on the open range in Montana. Fell off his horse, and broke his leg in three places. The horse run off, and he couldn't even get to his feet. Nobody went out to find him, and he laid there several days. When the turkey vultures got it figured out that he couldn't fight back, they came in on him. I rode up on him after it was over. I couldn't make out it was a man at first. They did a job on him.'

Davis turned and stared at him. 'You seen a lot out there.'

O'Brien sipped at his coffee. 'Like I told you. I know this ex-hunter down in Fort Revenge. Says he can put me on to some good trapping in that area. If not, I'll move on. Like I been doing most of my life.'

'I'm just saying. We ought to leave our options open. I remember one long summer in the Staked Plains. My mind was set on finding a big herd of buff. But then we heard about this bunch of mustangs running free in a box canyon.'

O'Brien held a hand up. 'Wait.'

Davis frowned at him. 'Huh?'

O'Brien stared hard out over the rolling plains, into a growing dusk. There was a slight rustling of wind in the nearby trees, and O'Brien's Appaloosa guffered quietly.

'What is it?'

'I thought I heard something. Out there.'

Davis shook his head, and grunted out a laugh. 'Come on, partner. You're always hearing things the rest of us don't. Relax and drink your coffee. Now, as I was saying about that one-horse town down south.'

Davis's head twitched slightly, and he frowned. In the distance, O'Brien heard a delayed rifle shot, and now saw three riders outlined on a remote hill. Davis put a hand up to his temple, still frowning, and felt a wetness there. His jaw started moving as if to speak, but no words came out. He turned to O'Brien quizzically, then fell on to his face into the fire.

O'Brien had risen from the log and was staring toward the riders, who were now galloping toward the camp. There was the increasing ground-shaking thunder of hoofbeats, and now O'Brien could see the riders plainly in the fading light. They were just a hundred yards away, and coming fast.

He never carried a sidearm; there were two rifles on his mount's irons which he hadn't yet removed for the night. In his right stove-pipe boot was a skinning knife in a rawhide sheath. He turned and started for the Appaloosa, as the riders dusted up just at the edge of his camp.

'I wouldn't do that, hunter,' the loud command came to him.

All three men had guns trained on him. Two had drawn revolvers, and the third one, a young man who appeared to be their leader, still held the long-distance Sharps rifle he had killed Davis with. O'Brien had one very much like it in one of his saddle scabbards. The one with the rifle was grinning.

12

'Well, well. Looks like we finally caught us some rustlers.'

O'Brien glared at him. Standing there by the fire, he looked very primitive, and wild. He exhibited no alarm at all. 'Are you the half-wit that killed my partner here?'

The rifleman's face went sober with that. The man on his right said, 'Let me have him. You got the other one.'

'No, no,' the first one replied. 'We ought to have some fun with this.'

'You call shooting a man down in cold blood fun?' O'Brien growled.

'I call shooting rustlers great entertainment,' was the arrogant response. He slid the rifle into its scabbard and dismounted. The other two, a beefy one and a rather slim fellow, followed suit.

'What do you think of that Sharps?' the younger man grinned, moving up to O'Brien. 'I took him from that far hill yonder.'

'Shooting a man at three hundred yards don't seem like nothing to be bragging about,' O'Brien countered. 'You afraid to get up close, cowboy?'

The other two still held their guns on him. The shooter came up nose to nose with O'Brien, but when he saw the look of him up close, some of the cockiness slid off his lean face. 'Is this close enough, trail bum?' he said rather loudly.

'You tell me,' O'Brien said in a low, easy tone.

'I'm Tully Purcell, mister,' the fellow went on. 'My daddy owns all this land for miles around, and you two thieves have been rustling his cattle for weeks now. We've been looking for a pair that fits your description for all that time, and now you stayed on just a little too long.'

'We're not rustlers,' O'Brien told him.

'Yeah, and the moon is made of Swiss cheese,' Purcell spat out. 'You're going to be the honored guest at a necktie

13

party under that cottonwood over there, mister. You like parties, don't you?'

'I think you ought to let it go,' O'Brien said. 'You already murdered an innocent man here tonight that you got to answer for.'

Purcell put a hand on the Colt Army revolver on his hip. 'I bet you got some gold hid around here somewhere. From when you sold our cattle.'

'I ain't got no gold. We're trappers. Here, look at this receipt for traps we bought in Abilene. That should show we ain't rustlers.'

Before Purcell could protest or draw the Colt, O'Brien reached casually to the boot sheath holding the skinning knife, slid the knife out, and thrust it upward into the mid-chest of Purcell, all in one fluid motion.

Tully Purcell's eyes saucered, and he was suddenly staring at O'Brien as if he were reacting to an insult. As he started to collapse, O'Brien grabbed him with one hand and snatched his revolver from its holster with the other. The lean companion reacted in shock and fired at O'Brien, but hit the dying Purcell in the back. O'Brien returned fire, that shot exploding riotously in the dark, and the lean man was punched in the chest just over the heart. He went running backwards wildly, firing again into a black sky before hitting the ground.

Now O'Brien released his hold on the dead Purcell, and trained the Colt on the hefty man. That fellow threw his gun to the ground as if it were a snake about to bite him, and raised his hands. 'Don't shoot!'

'Why not?' O'Brien growled.

'I didn't do no shooting. I never liked that rifle of Tully's.'

O'Brien walked over to him and placed the muzzle of the

gun against the other man's temple. 'That ain't a good enough reason to stop me from blowing the back of your head off.'

The fellow swallowed hard. 'What if I gave you some advice that just might save your life?' He was a Purcell ranch-hand, and his name was Lucas.

O'Brien just glared at him.

'You just killed Emmet Purcell's only boy. If I know Emmet, he'll ride to the ends of the Earth to find you. You ought to ride out of here tonight if you want to save your skin.' He watched O'Brien's hard eyes closely, sweat on his upper lip.

'You contaminated this place, swamp scum. When I get my partner buried, I intend to ride out. But you tell this Purcell that I killed that murdering son of his in self-defense. And that O'Brien don't run from nobody.' He removed the gun from the other man's head.

Lucas let out a long, uneven breath. 'O'Brien. Say, didn't you used to trade buffalo robes at the Fort Griffin Rendezvous?'

'What's that to you, you weasel?'

'We didn't know who you was.' Lucas said quietly.

'You didn't take time to ask,' O'Brien reminded him. He turned away, and went over and stared down at Davis, then pulled him out of the fire. 'Now get out of here before I change my mind.'

Lucas quickly loaded the Purcell kid and the other man aboard their mounts. It took a few minutes, and he was puffing when he finished. He tethered the other mounts to his own, and climbed back aboard just as O'Brien was done hauling Davis's body over to the trees. He intended to bury him there. Lucas turned to O'Brien soberly before he rode off. 'It won't make no difference to Purcell. That you wasn't

15

rustlers. Not with his boy dead. He'll come after you.'

O'Brien looked over at him. 'Mister, you got clabber for brains. If you're still here when I get this shovel from my gear, you better have an awful good reason.'

Lucas nodded uncertainly. He couldn't remember ever seeing a man so unconcerned for his own safety. 'Well. I'll just be heading back then.'

A few minutes later O'Brien was alone under the black sky. Off to the west, thunderheads were building, and the sky lighted up over there in a lightning flash that momentarily silhouetted the low trees and gnarled scrub of the desolate landscape. But no rain came. He worked for almost an hour putting Davis in the ground and saying a few words over him. Then he gathered up their gear, packed most of it on Davis's dun mare, and saddled up and rode off to the south.

He wanted to get away from this place of sudden, unreasoning death as soon as the Appaloosa could put it out of his sight.

He couldn't sleep tonight, anyway.

He would only dream of bald-headed, silly, talkative Davis, and that bewildered look he gave O'Brien just before he passed into eternity.

16

CHAPTER TWO

The Purcell ranch house was a large, rambling one, and was surrounded by several mesquite trees. When Wade Lucas rode in leading two horses with bodies thrown over their saddles, the ranch foreman Corey McGraw was standing on the long front porch, talking to two other ranch-hands. Lucas rode on into the yard, and they all narrowed their eyes on the somber parade of corpses before them.

'It's Tully!' Lucas called out. 'They killed him!'

McGraw's eyes narrowed even further, and he and a man next to him exchanged a look of disbelief. All three hurried off the porch to meet Lucas, who looked rather pale.

'They got Harris, too,' Lucas was saying as they gathered around him.

'Oh, no!' McGraw mumbled. 'Not Tully!'

'Who got them?' one of the others asked incredulously. 'What are you saying, Lucas?'

'The rustlers,' Lucas said. 'They killed Tully and Harris.'

In the next few minutes, the four of them hauled the two corpses off their mounts and brought them up on to the porch, everybody staring unbelievingly at the bodies.

'You better go get Emmet,' Lucas finally said to McGraw.

It was just a couple of moments later when Emmet

17

Purcell came rushing out on to the porch, face pale, eyes wide with disbelief. He was a tall fellow with gray hair, a tanned and weathered face, and a pot belly. He wore dungarees and a small leather vest over a work shirt. Now he stood over his dead son, his eyes watering up, his throat tight.

'Tully! My son!'

'The rustlers killed him,' McGraw told him. 'Him and Harris both.'

Purcell knelt down and touched Tully's lifeless face gently. Since his wife had died almost a decade ago, Purcell had spoiled his son badly, giving him anything he asked for, and demanding no responsibility or discipline in return. He finally rose, and turned to McGraw. 'Send somebody for the undertaker. We got to have us a funeral here, Corey.'

'I'm real sorry, Emmet,' McGraw said quietly. 'But we'll find them murderers if we have to chase them to China. You can rest easy on that score.'

Purcell sighed heavily. 'You and Lucas. Meet me in my den in ten minutes.'

'Yes, sir,' McGraw answered.

Tully's body was brought into the house and laid out on a dining room table; the other corpse was taken to the bunkhouse. After spending several more moments standing over his son's body, Purcell met with McGraw and Lucas in his big library room with its dark paneling and oriental carpeting, and row upon row of books that Purcell had never read. They all sat down on overstuffed chairs and a long sofa, and Purcell sat forward with his thick hands folded before him.

'Now, Lucas,' he finally began. 'You was there through all this?'

18

Lucas licked his dry lips. 'Yes, sir. Tully shot one of them with that new rifle you bought him. We was going to hang the other one. But he stuck a knife into Tully. Harris and me shot at him then,' he lied, 'but he used Tully as a shield.'

'You shot my son, too?' Purcell grated out.

Lucas could hardly speak. 'No, sir. That was Harris. The hunter killed Harris then, and got the drop on me. I had to throw my gun down.'

'You threw your gun down instead of killing the man who just shot Tully?' Purcell said ominously.

'He still held Tully,' Lucas lied again. 'I couldn't shoot past him, Emmet.' Watching Purcell's face closely. 'That's the truth of it.'

Purcell's face was hard. He finally looked away, kneading his hands. 'And these men were the ones that have been taking our cattle?'

Lucas sighed. 'Well. We never really established that.'

'What?'

Lucas looked sheepish. 'We just figured it was them. Tully shot from almost a quarter-mile away. He really liked that gun. But when the shooting was over, it turns out they might of been hunters.'

Purcell frowned. 'Hunters?'

'One of them was a man named O'Brien. He's the one that killed Tully and Harris.'

'O'Brien. Haven't I heard that name?'

'He's one of the old-time buff hunters. Looks more like a bear than a man. I heard stories about him. He's a mean one. Hard to put down in a fight. The Lakota made him one of them, I heard. I told him you'd come after him.'

Purcell stared past him, into some dark future. 'Is he still on my land?'

'I doubt it. I think he expected to ride out after he

19

buried his partner. I don't really think he rustled your cattle, Emmet. He ain't the type.'

'You can't know that,' McGraw finally spoke up, eyeing Purcell.

Purcell looked at him, then directed his hard gaze on Lucas again. 'My boy thought he was a rustler, and Tully had good judgment. Wouldn't you say, Lucas?'

Lucas hesitated, then nodded vigorously. 'Yes, sir.'

'Then as far as I'm concerned, this O'Brien has been stealing my cattle for the past several weeks. That gives me the right under the law to kill him.'

'Killing is too good for him,' McGraw said ominously.

'I think you're right, Emmet,' Lucas said nervously. 'I don't know what I was thinking. He was caught on your land. He kind of fits the description we got. And he killed the men who tried to apprehend him. He must be guilty.'

'He's guilty of murdering my only son,' Purcell said evenly. 'I don't need any more evidence than that.' He turned to McGraw. 'I'm putting you in charge of this, Corey. Get a more complete description of this O'Brien from Lucas, and tomorrow morning I want you to go out and see if you can pick up any trail. If he's a hunter, he'll probably be heading south into Indian Country. Let's find this murderer and send him to a fiery Hades. I won't rest easy till he's six feet under.'

'It will be my pleasure,' McGraw told him.

'Lucas, you tell that undertaker I want special treatment for my son. And I want him buried under that cottonwood out back, with his mother. He was the thing she lived and died for. I'm making a solemn vow to her, Corey, over her grave, that I'll make this right, that I won't quit till this O'Brien is six feet under, and we put him there. I'll use all my power and money to bring him down.'

20

'His death will be a memorial to Tully,' McGraw said in a hard voice.

'I'll go get the mortician,' Lucas said in a hushed tone.

Down in the Oklahoma Territory the following morning, in the small town of Fort Revenge, four men sat around a cutting table in the kitchen of the Prairie Café. They were a loosely organized gang of drifters and losers recently gathered together by Ben Driscoll, a thief and murderer wanted in three states to the north. With him in the kitchen were its owner, Maynard Quinn, who was about to go bankrupt; One-Eye Wylie, a bank robber from California; and Jake Latimer, a local farmer who had been involved in a few land swindles occasionally to make ends meet. It was Latimer who had applied to a Boston employment agency for a mail-order bride six months ago, in a fit of loneliness and woman-hunger, so she could keep house for him on his small farm. He had received notice just over two weeks ago that Sarah was on her way, but now that he had hooked up with Driscoll, he was sorry he had set all that machinery in motion, as it seemed ill-timed.

'When I got you boys together the last time, I started talking about how easy it might be to relieve some of the small banks in nearby towns of their ranch payrolls,' Driscoll was telling the others. They were alone in the kitchen, as Quinn had dismissed the help for the day.

'Yeah, I been thinking on that, Ben,' Quinn responded. 'That might not be as easy as we think. Banks around these parts are getting new fancy safes put in. It's a whole different world now. Used to be, a man could walk into a bank with a gun on him, ask for money, and walk out with his pockets full.' He had reddish hair and squinty eyes, and always wore a Homburg on the street. He was divorced and

21

a failure in business, and had met Driscoll in the restaurant. He wasn't as good with a gun as he imagined, but he had been in a saloon robbery as a younger man. He walked with a limp from a broken leg.

One-Eye Wylie, sitting across from him, grinned. 'What do you know about banks, fry cook? There ain't a bank in this whole Territory I couldn't take by myself, no other guns.' He was the other experienced gunman besides Driscoll. He had killed two men in a hold-up out in California, and was wanted for theft and murder in Missouri. He had straw-like hair and one good, dull-blue eye. The other one was scarred shut from a knife fight, and it gave him an unsettling look under his narrow-brim hat.

'Sure, Wylie. We know how tough you're supposed to be,' Quinn responded. 'You told us often enough.'

Wylie's pallid face colored. 'What does that mean, Apron Annie?'

'All right, boys,' Driscoll growled. 'We're not here to snipe at each other. We got business to discuss here.' He had premature silver hair and a lantern jaw. His eyes bore right through a man. His nose was broken in two places from saloon brawls, and he was very fast with his Remington .44, which he had 'sweetened' by filing the notch of the hammer. 'As I was about to say, I'm not here to talk about banks.'

The fourth man, Jake Latimer frowned at that. 'What's going on, Ben? Maynard here told me that was what you wanted to discuss with us. I got hogs to feed if you changed your mind.' He was leaning back on his chair arrogantly, and looked less like a farmer than anyone at the table except Wylie. He had inherited the small farm from an uncle, and had little interest in learning how to run it. He still hadn't turned a plow, and was selling off the livestock as fast as he could fatten it for market. He liked owning the farmhouse, though, and hoped to get a woman in it to take care of him and it, while he figured out a better way to make a living. He drank whenever he had the money for it, and thought that women were good only for cooking, cleaning, and in bed. One young Cherokee had kept house for him for a while, and acted as a wife to him, until he slapped her so hard it busted her right ear-drum, and she left him in the middle of a dark night.

Driscoll was irritated with his manner. 'Yes, I changed my mind, Latimer. You want to hear why, or just leave now?' he said in a low, grating voice.

Latimer arched his dark brows. He was considered good looking by women, and back in Arkansas where he came from, had been quite the ladies' man. 'I was just asking, Ben. I came here to hear you out.'

Driscoll gave him another hard look. 'I brought you people here to talk about that new stagecoach business here in town, the Territorial Express, run by some old buffalo hunter called Shanghai Smith.'

'I met him,' Quinn put in. 'Talks so loud he blows your hair back. Has all these stories about early buffalo hunting, talks a lot about Jim Elder, and a guy named O'Brien, and how they all roamed the northern plains together. Bores you to death.'

'I heard that name,' Wylie said darkly. 'O'Brien, not Smith. He made Bill Longley back down once in a saloon in Wichita, armed with just a Winchester rifle.'

'Can we get back to Smith?' Driscoll said in a threatening voice.

Wylie shot a one-eyed look at him. 'I was just commenting.'

Driscoll sighed. 'Smith has got a good thing going

23

here. He runs coaches to towns in all four directions, and business is booming. His passenger traffic alone pays his bills, I talked to his accountant. But now he's started hauling payrolls and gold deposits between banks around here.'

'Well, well,' Wylie said, leaning forward.

Latimer tipped a Stetson hat back on his head. 'I didn't know that!'

'Most folks don't,' Driscoll said. 'Which is why he hasn't had any hold-ups yet.'

Quinn stared over at his row of pots and pans hanging on a nearby wall, and rubbed his chin. 'You mean, you want to hit the coaches?'

'Why not?' Driscoll said. 'It's ten times easier than the banks. I figure we could hit them a half-dozen times before anybody gave us much trouble about it. And then we could all be rich, and retire to Mexico.'

'But all of us are well known around here,' Quinn said. 'They'd have a federal marshal on us as soon as he could ride here.'

'Yeah, it might be a one-time operation,' Latimer agreed.

Driscoll shook his head. 'I got that all figured out. It's Smith that knows us by sight. His drivers have never seen any of us up close. Anyway, all we have to do is shoot the driver, and then it's only passengers to worry over. And we'll all wear masks and long coats.'

Wylie nodded his head, his one eye looking a little brighter. 'I like it,' he announced. 'I like it a lot. I did one of these in California. There was a cash box aboard and every passenger had jewelry and money. We made a big haul, and it was like taking candy from a baby.'

'Count me in,' Latimer said, grinning.

Driscoll turned to his friend Quinn. 'Well, redhead? You

want a way out of the restaurant business? Or do you want to cook up beef stew the rest of your life?'

Quinn blew out his cheeks. 'I kind of like Smith.'

Driscoll gave him a look. 'Does that matter?'

'No. You're right,' Quinn said. 'This is business.'

'Good,' Driscoll said. 'I'll be in touch later about it.' He turned to Latimer. 'I hear you sent for a woman.'

Latimer nodded. 'That was before I met you, Ben. She's already on her way here.'

'I don't like that,' Wylie broke in.

Latimer turned coldly to him. 'Who asked you, little man?'

'Little man?' Wylie fumed. He was shorter than the rest of them.

'Wylie,' Driscoll warned him.

Wylie settled back on his seat, glaring at Latimer.

'Wylie has a point,' Driscoll continued. 'The woman adds a dimension to this – living with you; knowing your comings and goings.'

'She won't learn anything,' Latimer said.

'If she does, you know what you have to do.'

Latimer hesitated, then nodded. 'Yeah. I know. And I can handle it.'

'You better,' Driscoll said, holding his gaze with a somber one. 'You're betting your life on it.'

Latimer frowned at that threat. But you didn't argue with Driscoll. It just wasn't healthy. 'You can count on me, Ben,' he finally said.

'I still don't like it,' Wylie muttered to himself.

Quinn decided to break the tension. 'Why don't you boys all stick around to have some of my famous beef stew?' he grinned.

Driscoll rose from his chair. 'Maybe next time, Maynard,'

he said easily. 'I'm riding on back to my shack. I got big plans to make.'

CHAPTER THREE

By midday of the day after Curly Davis was killed by Tully Purcell, O'Brien was well into Indian Territory and far from the Purcell ranch. He had stopped under a low, gnarled pine in early morning, before the sun was up, and caught a short nap before fixing himself hot coffee and stuffing down the remaining corn dodgers left over from his last meal with Davis.

Now, with the sun high, he found himself out on a tree-less plain with many miles to go before he could reach any town, where he intended to sell Davis's horse and gear, and supply himself for the last push toward Fort Revenge. It was there his old friend and hunting partner Shanghai Smith might put him on to some favorable trapping grounds not overrun by reservation Indians.

He was getting ready to look for a decent place to make hardship camp soon, and make himself a real meal. His thoughts were on Davis and the people who had killed him. When he was younger, he would have shot the third man who was part of Davis's killing. He figured he had gone a bit soft in his early middle age, and that could be dangerous, out on the trail. But he had found it difficult to pull the trigger on a sweating fool like Lucas.

He spurred the Appaloosa onward to the top of a low hill, with Davis's mare following along behind, when he spotted the small creek off to the left. But then something else caught his eye.

About twenty yards from the creek was a wagon with its team missing, and the ground surrounding it was littered with scraps of cloth and clothing. On the box seat of the wagon a woman sat, ramrod-erect, wearing a Boston-bought dress and holding a parasol over her head, as if she were waiting for a horse-drawn cab to come and take her to some planned tea party.

O'Brien stared in disbelief. Images like this just didn't present themselves on the plains of the Indian Territory. He looked around carefully, making sure this wasn't an ambush of some kind. There was no other sign of life anywhere around the wagon, or the creek but over by the creek, turkey vultures wheeled high overhead, staring down at something dead in the high rushes.

O'Brien slid his Winchester rifle out of its scabbard on the Appaloosa's flank. In addition to the other rifle, a Sharps, he also carried a Schofield .45 revolver in a saddle wallet, but he prefered the long gun for defense.

He spurred the stallion again, and both horses continued on down the slope toward the wagon, with O'Brien watching warily in all directions. As he approached closer to the wagon, Sarah Carter turned, saw him, and screamed.

He rode on up to the wagon, peering inside it for a moment. Then he came around to face Sarah. 'No need for alarm, ma'am. I'm just a hunter on my way south. What are you doing here?'

She had shied away from him. Now she slowly relaxed. She had tried to sleep through the night after the killings, and early this morning she had resolved to just sit and wait

28

for help, hoping that it came before a return of the Pawnee. She hadn't heard O'Brien's approach, and he had scared her badly.

'We were attacked by Indians,' she said, studying the wild-looking man before her.

'Where's your driver?'

'There were two of them. They were both killed. I was down at the creek there, and they never found me.' Some of her dark hair had blown loose alongside her face, and there was a small smudge of dirt on her cheek.

O'Brien looked again out over the rolling terrain, squinting into the sun. 'You was mighty lucky, ma'am. Them arrows look like Pawnee. They ain't the kind to treat a white woman with much respect. Is that the dead drivers them vultures is circling over?'

She nodded. 'I dragged them into the weeds last night, so I wouldn't have to look at them.'

O'Brien liked that. 'I see you got some grit, lady.'

'I've been terrified they'd come back. When I heard you, I thought they had. Thank God you found me, mister. You're the answer to my prayers.'

'Why don't we hold off judgment on that?' he said easily. He dismounted and tethered the Appaloosa to the wagon, and walked around to look in it again, at its rear. 'I see they cleaned you out pretty good.'

'My trunk is still there, with most of my things in it. I guess they weren't very interested in women's belongings.'

'I see they left a box of hardtack, too, and a few tins of fruit. Indians ain't much for canned goods.'

Sarah climbed down off the seat of the wagon and came around to join him. He now got a close-up look at her and was surprised by her genteel good looks, and her age. Most women alone in the West were quite young.

'I don't mean to pry, ma'am, but was one of them drivers your husband?'

'Oh, no,' she said. 'That's why I'm traveling to Oklahoma. To get married there.'

O'Brien frowned slightly. 'You didn't answer one of them ads for a mail-order wedding?'

She blushed. 'Yes, I did. Why? Do you find something wrong with that?'

'I don't try to work out what's right for other folks,' he said. 'Well, I better get them two freight men in the ground. I got a shovel on my mount's irons. Where was you headed from here?'

'I'm going to Fort Revenge, a little town in the Territory. I'm committed to a farmer there, and hope to make a new life with him.'

O'Brien grunted out a small laugh. 'Well, if that don't beat all. I'm heading down there myself.' He walked to his horse, pulled a shovel from its saddlery, and headed for the high reeds.

It took him a while to make a hole deep enough to bury both men, but finally he returned to the wagon, where Sarah had opened a can of peaches and put some in a tin cup for him. They ate the canned fruit in silence. O'Brien then wiped his mouth on a rawhide sleeve as he finished.

'Real good, ma'am. Haven't had nothing like that since Abilene.'

'Glad you liked them. I'm Sarah Carter.'

He nodded. They were leaning against the sideboard of the wagon.

'Call me O'Brien.'

'Just O'Brien?'

'That's right, ma'am.'

She smiled, relaxed now. She was beginning to like the

look of this primitive man. 'I'm glad we're going to the same place, O'Brien. Maybe we can travel together.'

He looked over at her with a solemn gaze. 'Oh, no, ma'am. I travel fast and live hard. There's a town up ahead a short ride from here, called Barrow's Corner. We can be there tomorrow morning. I'll drive the wagon that far, and you can get a stagecoach there to Fort Revenge.'

She was disappointed. She was feeling safe with him. 'I can ride a horse, O'Brien. I learned how at a riding academy in Boston when I was still in school.'

O'Brien sighed. 'It ain't quite the same out here, ma'am. As you found out just yesterday.'

'Please call me Sarah.'

'All right. Sarah. You see, there's all kinds of hardships out here on the trail; some you can foresee and plan on, and some that take you by surprise. I wouldn't want the responsibility, ma'am.'

She stiffened slightly. 'I see.'

'Now, I'm going to hitch these two horses to your wagon, and drive you on into Barrow's Corner. There'a a little hotel there that will put you up till the next stage comes through. With a little luck, you'll arrive at Fort Revenge not long after me.'

She nodded reluctantly. 'Very well.'

By mid-afternoon O'Brien had the two horses hitched to the freight wagon. The mare took to the harness without trouble, but the Appaloosa kicked and reared until O'Brien reassured it. O'Brien helped Sarah up on to the wagon seat again and they rode up there together as he got the new team moving, the rolling terrain slipping slowly past. About an hour before sunset, O'Brien found a shady spot along the same small stream, under willow trees, and parked the wagon and made a fire for them.

31

Sarah was eager to help, and while he took the horses down to the water, she boiled some of his coffee over their fire. There was a stool in the wagon, and O'Brien brought that out for her to sit on, while he settled for his mount's saddle. They hadn't talked much through the afternoon, and not at all about themselves. Now O'Brien found some flour from Davis's belongings, and the grease they had saved from the salt pork, and Sarah baked some biscuits in an oven made from field stones. O'Brien burnt some more pork over the fire, and Sarah had her first hardship camp meal. She didn't complain, and that pleased O'Brien. It was dark by the time they got the hardware cleaned up and put away, and O'Brien made up a bed for her in the wagon, and spread his own bedroll out near the fire. Then they sat and drank some more coffee.

'Did you say you're a hunter, O'Brien?' she finally said to him.

He nodded. 'Well, I was, Sarah. Buffalo mostly, but the shaggies are cleaned out now. Now I hunt for meat. And do some trapping.'

'You trap animals?'

'Yeah. Beaver. Ermine. Some fox. The hides bring pretty good pay at the town markets.'

She absorbed that for a moment. 'I don't think I could trap and kill an animal,' she observed.

O'Brien looked over at her. 'I reckon we do a lot of things out here that folks might shy away from in Boston,' he said. 'But I guess even in your state the farmers raise live-stock for grub and leather. And folks in fancy restaurants eat their steaks done to order, wearing their polished shoes and carrying their hand-made purses without having to go to the trouble of actually butchering a cow, or tracking a mule deer for an hour in the snow, only to find a bear already killed and ate most of it; or checking traps in an ice-cold stream till your hands freeze up so bad you can't unpicket your horse with them.'

Sarah met his sober look. 'I'm sorry. That was an insensitive thing to say. I didn't mean to demean your occupation.'

O'Brien had never heard the word 'demean'. He turned to the fire. 'Sarah, we ain't hunting and trapping for sport out here. Some of us do it just to make it through another day, or another year. If we wasn't going to hit Barrow's Corner in the morning tomorrow, I'd be looking for something to shoot for our camp-fire. Death is part of life out here – for the animals, and for us.'

Sarah had never heard anybody talk like that. But everything he said had a ring of truth in it. 'I guess I was brought up in a protected setting,' she admitted. 'I fed squirrels and put bird feeders out. And I am one of those people who ordered steaks and roasts at restaurants. I even bought a set of leather luggage a year ago, planning to make a trip to Charleston. But my last parent got sick and died, my aging father, and the expenses took most of what I had saved. I even had to sell the luggage. That trunk in the wagon was all I could afford this time.'

O'Brien usually hated to sit and talk with anyone. Nobody ever seemed to have anything of interest to say. But Sarah, he decided, was different. Maybe he had forgotten how different women were. He liked the melodic sound of her voice; for some reason, it was soothing to him. Unlike listening to Curly Davis, or Shanghai Smith, this was quite pleasant.

'I guess you was never married.'

'That's right. I was engaged once, but it didn't work out. I think maybe he loved himself more than me.' She gave him a little smile 'I took a job at our library. Did a lot of reading. But that doesn't take the place of living, does it?'

'Couldn't tell you, Sarah. Never learned to read much. Had a riding partner once that used to read the Kansas City paper to me. Me, I can't make out a lot of it.'

Sarah turned to look at him more carefully. That speech had touched her. 'If we had more time, I could teach you to read.'

O'Brien grunted. 'I don't miss it, ma'am. I get my news by word of mouth, the stuff that's important to me. I ain't much interested in who's running Mexico now, or whether the Capitol in Washington's got any electricity. Them things is for men of importance, folks that run the world.'

'You're a man of importance,' Sarah said.

He glanced at her sidewise.

'Men like you have tamed the West for settlement. I don't see what could be more important than that. Anyway, reading is more than the news. There are stories that inspire, and beautiful poetry. Have you done this all your life?'

'Most of it. I was out in the woods shooting game for the table when I was eight. That was back in Tennessee. My daddy taught me to shoot. I was trading with the Cherokee when I was ten, and killed my first bear at fourteen.'

Sarah sneaked another look at the bearded, rugged-looking man sitting near her at the fire, and realized for the first time how fortunate she had been when he had stumbled on to her wagon earlier.

'You must have been close to your father,' she suggested.

'We hunted together for years. Never had no real trouble with him except for one time. We had an old hound that used to go out with us. The hound got sick, and my daddy went out to shoot him one night. I got my eight-gauge and stood between him and the dog, and said if he shot Willy,

34

I'd shoot him.'

Sarah was frowning. 'What did he do?'

'He backed off. I think he believed me. I wouldn't have shot him, but I wouldn't never spoke to him again. The dog got well, and lived for another three years.'

Sarah sat there and mulled all of that. 'That's a remarkable story.'

O'Brien was surprised and sorry that he had opened up so much. It was very unlike him. 'I guess I ran off at the mouth a little there.'

'I enjoyed the story immensely. It was very provocative.'

He looked up at her. 'Sarah. I know you been educated, and you read a lot of books. But you'll have to tone it down a little out here, or nobody's going to know what you're saying.'

She flushed slightly. 'Oh, I'm sorry. I see what you mean. I'll try harder.'

'No offense meant, ma'am. I just want you to fit in. Things will be hard enough for you when you get to Fort Revenge.'

'You think this was a bad idea, don't you?'

'Out here, Sarah, we try to keep out of other folks' business. But a contract to marry a man you never seen might not work out just the way you hope. Especially down here in the Territory.'

'Why especially here?'

'Well, ma'am. You see, all the misfits and law-breakers in the West tend to end up in the Territory. They're all running from something, and there ain't hardly no law at all around here. Maybe a half-dozen federal marshals to cover the whole Territory, and a judge in Stillwater, and that's it.'

'But I committed myself to a farmer, O'Brien. A responsible citizen who just wants to make a family life for himself.'

O'Brien nodded. 'I understand. Don't pay me no mind, ma'am. I'm just a cautious man. I'm sure everything will be all right for you. I'll be in town there on a regular basis if things work out for me, so if I see you on the street, I'll say hey.'

She was smiling again. 'I'd like that.'

'Now maybe we ought to try to get some sleep,' he concluded, rising off his saddle. Out on the plain, there was a long, wailing sound.

'What was that?' Sarah asked nervously.

'Just a coyote, ma'am,' he said. 'Don't worry, he won't bother us none. We'll just keep our grub out of his reach. He's smart, sometimes smarter than us.'

Sarah was on her feet. 'I meant to ask you. Do you always ride alone?'

'Mostly. But I did have a partner till a couple days ago.'

She frowned. 'What happened?'

'Oh, he was killed by ranchers. Mistook us for rustlers.'

She gasped slightly. 'Oh, heavens! That's terrible!'

'Yes, ma'am. But things like that do happen.'

'How did you survive that?' she wondered.

'Oh, I had to take a couple of them down,' O'Brien replied casually, as if reporting that his Appaloosa had thrown a shoe.

'You mean, you killed them?' she asked, wide-eyed.

'Yes, ma'am. Well, I'll just go make sure the horses is getting along all right. That mare looked kind of tired when we got here.'

Then he turned and walked away toward the picketed horses, with Sarah staring after him as if he had just told her that Mexico had declared war on the US.

'Good heavens,' she repeated, under her breath.

She was learning more about this strange man with every hour that passed.

And she wasn't at all sure she wanted to know more.

Wade Lucas and his foreman McGraw had been trying to find O'Brien's trail all this time, but without success. They had picked it up that next morning after the shootings at the campsite where it all happened, and had been able to follow it for a few hours, until another trail joined the one O'Brien was following, and O'Brien's tracks merged with many others, and they lost them.

Figuring the hunter might have detoured to a small town off to the east a few miles, they followed that hunch and ended up in Dry Junction about the same time that O'Brien had discovered Sarah Carter on down the trail. Now they were asking around town about O'Brien, hoping he was there or had been there. About the time that O'Brien and Sarah were bedding down out on the trail, Lucas and McGraw were having a late meal in the dining room of a small inn in Dry Junction, and discussing future plans.

Lucas took a last forkful of roast beef from his plate and chewed on it vigorously. 'I say we ought to go back and report what we know. Emmet might have different plans now.'

'What plans can he make when we don't know nothing?' McGraw said irritably. 'That hunter could be headed for west Texas, or off east to Little Rock. He must know we're coming after him, you know. He could even have headed south just to throw us off, and be circled around now and riding for Kansas. Is that what you want to tell Emmet if we go back now?'

Lucas shrugged. 'He might have some ideas.'

'I don't think you know Emmet, boy. You go back and tell

37

him we lost O'Brien, he might just take you out to the barn and give you twenty lashes to give you some incentive. I seen him whip a new hand just for spilling hot soup on his new boots. You're lucky he didn't put a bullet in you for coming back alive from that shoot-out. He ain't a forgiving man.'

'I seen his bullwhip,' Lucas muttered, 'hanging in the stable. How many lashes did he give that new man?'

'That ain't the point!' McGraw fairly yelled at him, throwing his napkin down. They were finished now with their meal. 'I'm saying, you don't ride back to the ranch just to tell Emmet we failed. He wants to hear we caught the hunter and put him six feet under. That's the only report he'll listen to. No, we keep looking now, till we get some clue about where that killer went.'

'But we don't even know what direction to ride in,' Lucas protested. He was a messy-looking man, with stringy hair sticking out from under his hat. His build was stocky, and his belly stuck out some over his belt. 'What do we do next?'

McGraw sighed. He was a broad-coupled fellow, with a square, weathered face and some gray at his temples. He had been with Purcell for almost fifteen years. He always wore a Confederate States belt buckle on his gunbelt, and spoke in a gravelly, southern accent. 'We keep looking. This town is east of the trail he started out on, and nobody's seen him here, so I'm going to figure he ain't riding east. Now we'll ride over west to another little berg I know there, and ask around. If we get the same answers there, I'm going to figure he's on his way south. In that direction, he'd hit Barrow's Corner and then go through Sulphur Creek on the way to Fort Revenge or Tulsa. We'll check them all out.'

'What if he fooled us and headed north?'

'Then we better never go back to the Purcell ranch,' McGraw said soberly. 'I wouldn't want to face Emmet in the mood he'd be in.'

Lucas thought about that for a long moment. 'Why did we have to find them hunters out there, anyway?' Then to himself: 'Why couldn't we have stayed back at the bunkhouse that night?'

'Why did them two steal Emmet's cattle?' McGraw countered. 'Why did Emmet buy Tully that long gun? I don't know why things happen. They just do.'

'Them two didn't steal Emmet's cattle,' Lucas said quietly.

McGraw gave him a hard look. 'Don't ever say that again, boy. In fact, get that right out of your head. As far as we're concerned, them hunters is as guilty as sin. You think any other way, it could cost you your life.'

Lucas eyed him narrowly, not knowing exactly what he meant by that. 'OK. I'll remember that,' he said in a subdued tone.

'Now, let's go get us some sleep,' McGraw said in a tired voice. 'We got to ride clear over to Little Gulch tomorrow to do the same thing there.'

Lucas nodded. His heart wasn't in this. He had met O'Brien briefly a few years ago at the big Fort Griffin Rendezvous, where traders, hunters, and trappers came from hundreds of miles around to do business with each other. He had spoken to Indians and mountain men about O'Brien, and none had had a bad word to say about the hunter, except that he exhibited an aloof manner, and never joined in the palavers around the camp-fires.

O'Brien, he knew, was no more a rustler than himself. But if Emmet Purcell said he was, that made it an indisputable fact. And he also knew that if he had to kill O'Brien to keep on the good side of Purcell, he wouldn't hesitate a minute.

O'Brien didn't know it yet, but he was a walking dead man.

CHAPTER FOUR

It was a bright, sunny day when Sarah Carter and O'Brien drove the freight wagon into Barrow's Corner, and the weather had warmed up. The little patches of snow that had spotted the plains from the hard winter were finally gone, and flocks of geese could be seen flying north on their migration routes. In town, women were on the street without coats, and windows had been thrown open.

The town was small, but it had a bank, a general store, and a saloon. There was also a hotel called the Trail's End. The first thing that took O'Brien's notice, though, was the old stagecoach building that was all boarded up, down at the far end of town.

'That don't look good,' he muttered.

'Isn't that where the stage stops?' Sarah asked him.

'I don't see no other place,' O'Brien offered. 'Maybe it stops at the hotel nowadays. We better go check it out.'

They turned the team around, drove back to the hotel, and parked out in front. O'Brien got off the wagon. 'You rest easy and let me ask,' he told her. 'I'll be right back out.'

Sarah looked dispirited. Nothing seemed to be going right. 'All right, O'Brien. I'll wait here.'

O'Brien climbed some steps and entered the hotel lobby.

40

There were a couple of potted palms that looked withered, and a long reception desk that filled most of the back wall. Behind the desk was a bank of key boxes, and a painting by Remington, of Apaches in hunting gear. The place smelled like ammonia.

There was also a narrow doorway behind the desk, and a clerk now emerged, hearing O'Brien's riding spurs clinking on the hardwood floor.

'Yes, sir. Can I help you?' He was thin and emaciated-looking, and wore rimless spectacles. He looked O'Brien over with disdain.

'I see the stage company's place is shut down, and thought maybe they was using the hotel to let off passengers nowadays.'

The clerk made a sour face. 'Oh, no. We wouldn't do that. That line don't come this way anymore. I think it went completely out of business.'

'You mean there's no transportation south from here at all?'

A smug grin. 'None at all, mister. But you look like a man that could ride his own mount out of here.'

O'Brien sighed. 'I got a woman outside. She has to get to Fort Revenge. Could she hire a private coach or carriage to get her that far?'

'Not a chance. She could try at Dry Junction. But the stage don't go through there either.'

'That would be a day's ride in the wrong direction,' O'Brien frowned. 'Are you trying to hooraw me a little bit here, flea-brain?' he said ominously.

The clerk's demeanor changed, and he backed up a step, without knowing he had done so. 'I didn't mean no disrespect, stranger.' He looked O'Brien over with a heavy frown. 'Look, maybe you and your woman would be more comfortable somewhere else. I can direct you to a nice little boarding house down the road a piece.'

O'Brien sighed, then walked around to the rear of the counter where the clerk stood. He studied the key boxes. 'You got anything on the first floor?'

'Excuse me, you can't be back here!' the clerk protested weakly.

O'Brien found a first floor key, and showed it to the clerk. 'This one ought to be fine.'

'We hold that room for special guests,' the clerk blurted out.

'The other ones are on the second floor. The lady wants the first floor.'

'I told you. That's reserved.'

O'Brien grabbed hold of the clerk's vest and spoke to him nose to nose. 'How often do them important people come through this backwater town?' he said in a low growl.

The clerk was suddenly breathless. 'Why, not very often, I guess.'

'Then like I said. We'll take this room.'

The clerk nodded, gasping. 'Yes, sir.'

O'Brien released him. 'We'll be back.' He was in a foul mood now.

Outside in the sun, two young men had approached the wagon and were talking to Sarah, who now sat with her parasol over her head again.

'Come on, lady,' the slimmer one was urging. They gave the appearance of local ranch-hands. 'It's right down the street there. Come on and deal a few hands of Dueces Wild for us. Women bring me luck.'

The other man was more brawny, and had a three-day growth of beard. 'Yeah, get down from there, girlie. Or I'll help you down.'

Sarah saw O'Brien emerge from the hotel and come down the steps, and was very relieved. 'Oh, O'Brien. You're back.'

O'Brien came on over to the wagon, still irritated. The two men turned to look him over, and the brawny one grinned. 'Hey. I think I smell the stink of buffalo. Is this your driver, honey?'

'Go find a cow to punch,' O'Brien said curtly to him. 'The lady and me got business to talk here.'

'Business?' the brawny one said. 'I think we got first call on that, buffalo dung. Now why don't you go get yourself a bath and give us a little elbow room here?'

O'Brien was suddenly very fed up with smart-talking locals, and impatient to explain the situation to Sarah. He turned casually to the brawny man and threw an iron-hard fist into his face. Bone snapped audibly in the fellow's nose and cheek, and then he hit the ground hard on his back, out cold. His leg twitched once and he lay stone still. O'Brien turned to the other man, who raised his hands defensively.

'Hey, wait! We was just funning, mister!' he said hoarsely.

'Haul his carcass out of my sight,' O'Brien grated out.

A moment later the slim man was dragging his limp cohort toward a nearby store canopy. Sarah stared hard at O'Brien now. 'Did you really have to do that?'

O'Brien shook his head and studied the ground for a moment. 'Look, Sarah. I fixed you up with a room at the hotel. I figure you'll be better off staying here a day or two, and hitching a ride with somebody else. I'm thinking of you, Sarah.'

'There isn't anybody I could ride with that I would feel as safe with as I do with you,' she told him.

He looked over at her.

43

'You have to take me, O'Brien. Please.'

He sighed. 'I'll just go get your trunk off the wagon, Sarah,' he said.

She turned away from him, tears in her eyes. O'Brien hauled her trunk off the back of the wagon, and carried it up the steps and into the lobby of the hotel, where the clerk eyed it distastefully. Then O'Brien was back at the wagon.

'Your room is waiting for you,' he said.

She avoided eye contact as he helped her off the wagon. Since the Indians had attacked the wagon, she was afraid all the time, and only O'Brien had relieved that fear. Now she would be on her own again. He took her into the hotel and the desk clerk registered her. Then O'Brien turned to her.

'This is the best thing for you, you know.'

She wouldn't look into his eyes. 'If you say so.'

'There's a dining room here for eats,' he said. 'I'll go sell your wagon and the mare, and be right back. Then I'll be riding out.'

She took the key and walked away from him.

In the next hour or so, O'Brien sold the wagon and mare for a decent price, and returned to the hotel. It was past noon now. He saw a pinto stallion hitched outside at the rail, and figured a new guest had arrived. But when he got to Sarah's room, he found out it was hers.

'You bought a horse?' he frowned at her.

'That's right. I told the clerk I'm not staying. I'm riding on south today.'

O'Brien was frustrated. He laid a wad of paper money on a chest of drawers near her. 'You can't do that, Sarah. Here's your money – I got you a good deal. Pay the clerk for the night and wait for a freight wagon to come through.'

'I have to make my own decisions now,' she told him. She had cleaned up, and she looked pretty to him. 'If I'm going

44

to live out here in the West, I'm going to have to learn how to take care of myself.'

He pulled his trail-colored Stetson off and hurled it on to the bed nearby. 'You're making a plumb fool of yourself, ma'am. Women that have lived here all their lives don't go riding off into the prairie by themselves.' His long, wild hair was shaggy-looking, and his blue eyes flashed anger. 'Now, you pay attention to what I'm telling you. You got to stay on here in Barrow's Corner till you can get transportation south.'

'I don't have to do anything I don't want to do,' she retorted, 'or be concerned about what anybody else wants for me. I've pared down my belongings so they fit into this small bag here that will fit on my horse's flanks, and I'll leave the trunk here. I'm sure the hotel clerk will find some use for it.'

O'Brien turned away, fuming inside. Men didn't argue with O'Brien, and if they did, they lost. This was different. 'I should have left you out there on that wagon,' he muttered to himself. 'You been nothing but trouble, lady.'

'I'm not your trouble any more. Now, if you'll excuse me, O'Brien. I'm doing some last-minute packing to leave.' She faced him boldly, her chin set.

O'Brien turned back to her, and his face softened. 'All right,' he said.

She turned and frowned at him. 'What?'

'All right, you can ride with me.'

A beautiful smile spread over her face. 'Really?'

He looked her over. 'What do you expect to wear?'

'There's a pair of riding pants in my things, and knee boots.'

'We'll have to buy you a hat for the sun, down the street. Well, get your stuff packed up and I'll go get the hat. Don't

45

pack too much. Remember, your horse has to carry it.'

'I won't.' She felt better at this moment than she had on the entire trip. 'I appreciate this, O'Brien.'

'Don't thank me. I ain't doing you no favors, Sarah. I'll be right back.'

Despite his curtness of manner and frequent lack of civility, Sarah liked him very much. He exuded a powerful force around him, and she needed that feeling right now. 'I'll be ready.'

O'Brien bought her a narrow-brim, light brown Stetson, and she liked the feel of it on her. Within the hour they were packed and loaded, and O'Brien had looked her pinto over. It was smaller than the Appaloosa, but appeared to be a strong animal. She had chosen well at a corral behind the hotel.

He watched her board her mount with interest, and was pleased to see that she wasn't awkward about it. But he knew she would be very sore when this day's ride was finished. And then she would have to do it all over. When they were both mounted, she looked over at him.

'Well, O'Brien,' she said with a big smile, 'let's put some miles behind us.'

O'Brien regarded her somberly. 'I reckon you don't own a gun?'

She was surprised. 'Why, of course not.'

'I got a Schofield I can loan you. I'll fix it on your mount's irons the first time we stop. You can shoot a revolver, can't you?'

'Yes. But why would I want a gun?'

'You never know why you need it till you need it,' he said. 'I won't be with you every minute. You'll need protection.'

'If you say so,' she said. She no longer looked like a Boston librarian, with the riding clothes and Stetson. But

O'Brien knew it was all looks at this point. 'Now can we go?' she added pleasantly.

O'Brien made a face, and shook his head. He felt like a fool for getting involved with this Boston lady and her western adventure. 'Yeah,' he said disconsolately. 'Let's ride out.'

CHAPTER FIVE

Shanghai Smith sat on the small porch of his stagecoach headquarters at the far edge of town in Fort Revenge, staring out over the rolling countryside and remembering the good old days of buffalo hunting. Above his head hung his company sign, which read, TERRITORIAL EXPRESS. He was a mountain of a man, standing several inches over six feet and weighing close to three hundred pounds. What hair he still had was gray, and he had a broad, meaty face with ruddy cheeks. He wore a grizzled beard that looked much like O'Brien's. He was studying a bill of lading now, and to do so had placed a small pair of spectacles down on the end of his pudgy nose.

He turned his head toward the open door behind him. 'Hey, Foley! Did you write this bill?'

After a moment a small, wiry man emerged from inside. Smith was short on drivers now, since one of them had quit recently to join a brother-in-law up in Kansas City. Foley had rheumy eyes and a sour-looking mouth. He walked a bow-legged walk over to Smith, and squinted down at the paper Smith held.

'Yep. That's the Johnson bill. He shipped some green turnips with us. Sells them to some grocer down in Stillwater.'

48

'Well, he didn't sign this,' Smith said in his booming voice. 'Did you ask him?'

Foley shrugged. 'Who knows? I think he got to talking about his goats and just forgot.' He pulled up a second straight chair beside Smith and stared out over the dry landscape. 'I'll get him next time.'

Smith shook his head, and let the paper drop to his lap. He had been one of the best known of the buffalo hunters in his day. He went way back to when the plains were black with them, and men shot them out of train windows, and other men came clear over from Europe to kill them for sport. They and the big hide companies had almost spoiled it for lone professional hunters, but men like Smith and O'Brien had made a living at it for quite a while before it all came to an end. When it was over, it was the loners like Smith and O'Brien and Jim Elder and the Sioux who paid the price for other men's greed.

'You got a run down to Stillwater in a half-hour,' Smith said. 'You got that team ready out back?'

'I just got to harness them up,' Foley said. 'I got a lunch all packed up, too. We got a couple of passengers sitting inside, waiting to go.'

'I saw them,' Smith boomed out. 'I'm expecting a couple more, too. If things keep going like this, we're going to have us a real business here.'

'I know you give me a shotgun to keep up with me on the box,' Foley said pensively. 'But you know, Shanghai, we really need a man to ride shotgun. You can't see what's coming up on you when you're driving the team. Down near Tulsa, a stage was held up, and the driver killed. That could happen to us. And it don't help none that we ain't got us a town marshal here.'

'You know I put up a broadside,' Smith replied. 'It ain't

49

that easy to find somebody nowadays. I'm glad to have three other drivers now, for most of our routes. You're lucky you ain't got that Sulphur Creek run. That's a lot of rough trail.'

Foley sat there. 'Another thing. That gambler Ben Driscoll. He's been here a couple of times studying our schedule. But he don't never buy a ticket.'

'You can't blame him for that, Foley.'

'It's just the way he does it. I also saw him looking my coach over the other day. Why all the interest?'

'Maybe he's going to start up a second line here,' Smith guessed.

'That's all we'd need to put us out of business,' Foley said acidly.

Smith looked over at him. 'You're like a hog rooting in a bucket for something to worry over,' he declared. 'Just drive your route and let me figure out what trouble might be coming at us. I been in shaggy stampedes so wild I had to find a hole to hide in, and I lived through blue northers where the wind was blowing so hard it impaled farmers to trees with their own pitchforks. I reckon I can handle business competition without losing my head.'

Foley shrugged. 'We need some people to ride shotgun,' he insisted. 'That's all I'm saying.'

Across town in a small shack off the main trail to Tulsa, Driscoll and his new companions, One-Eye Wylie and Jake Latimer, were discussing Shanghai Smith at that very moment.

Driscoll had erected a poster board on a wall near a fireplace that didn't work, and had tacked up a map of the Oklahoma Territory on it. He was standing in front of the map, while Wylie and Latimer were seated at a rough-hewn table a few feet away. Their fourth partner, Maynard Quinn was busy at his restaurant.

'Now this is the place I'm talking about,' he was saying, pointing to a mark on the map not far from Fort Revenge. 'This is on the route down to Stillwater. I think that dumb-bell Foley drives it. As you know, Wylie, when you get out of town about an hour there's an area of high rocks, and a narrow pass. That would be a perfect place to ambush Smith's stage.'

'I been out that way,' Wylie said, his scarred eye-socket glistening in the sunlight from a window. 'There's a high ridge on the east side of the trail that the stage passes right under. We could ride blind out of there and be right on top of them. They wouldn't know what hit them.'

'That's the point I was making,' Driscoll said. He looked over to Jake Latimer, who was slouched on his chair looking uninterested. 'Latimer. You got any comments?' He hadn't been pleased with his choice of Latimer from the beginning.

Latimer pursed his lips. He was disliked by every farmer in the area because he sat on a farm without working it. He had expected Sarah Carter's arrival in town by now, and had let the farm house become a mess. He had sold off all his livestock, and also some extra acres, and intended to live on the proceeds until his partnering up with Driscoll could make some money for him. Latimer had never really done a hard day's work in his life, and didn't expect to.

'I don't like it, Ben. It sounds tricky, coming down out of them rocks. I like the Tulsa run better, it's all level ground for riding, and there's a stand of cottonwoods about ten minutes out of town we could hide in. It makes more sense.'

'And my plan don't make sense?' Driscoll said, his face suddenly dark-looking.

'It ain't smart, Ben. Why over-exert ourselves to knock

51

over a second-rate, back-country stagecoach when we might end up with small change, anyway? It just ain't smart.'

Driscoll's expression had grown even more fierce. He sighed, walked over to Latimer at the table, and drew the Remington .44 from his hip. He stuck it up to Latimer's temple. 'Now how smart do you feel, pig farmer?' In a low growl.

Latimer froze. 'Hey. Take it easy, Ben!'

'I don't like your smart ideas, Latimer. I don't like you. Maybe I just ought to put a bullet in your brain and find me somebody else to help out on this.'

'No, wait, Ben,' he said tightly, tongue suddenly clicking on a dry mouth. 'I didn't mean to get crossways of you. I just wanted to throw some ideas out.'

'Blow his ear off,' Wylie said from nearby, grinning.

Driscoll's finger was tight over the trigger. 'I don't want your stupid ideas, pig farmer. You ain't running this show.'

'That's right,' Latimer said quickly, his handsome face ashen. 'You are, Ben. We all know that.'

Driscoll hauled off and slugged Latimer across the side of the head with the Remington, almost knocking him off the chair. Latimer gasped in shock, his breath coming raggedly.

Driscoll hesitated a moment, then holstered the gun. 'Now you keep your lame-brain ideas to yourself from now on, and I just might keep you on the payroll. A man like you ought to just sit and listen to others. You might learn something.'

'You might just learn something,' Wylie echoed him.

Driscoll gave Wylie a hard look, and walked back to the map. Latimer sat there holding his head, blood inching down the side of his face. He had just lost most of his arrogance for good. And he had found out you make a special effort to keep on the good side of Ben Driscoll.

'Now, as I was saying before,' Driscoll said, as if nothing had happened. 'We'll hit that stage right here. And that Foley. I think he might have seen me studying their schedule yesterday. Soon as we ride out on them, Wylie, that will be your first job: put one in Foley's head.'

By early afternoon that day, O'Brien and Sarah Carter were well on their way south. O'Brien figured that if they rode hard and didn't spend much time eating, they could be in Sulphur Creek by nightfall. It was the last town on the trail until they reached Fort Revenge.

Sarah surprised O'Brien with her stamina and resolve. In several hours of riding she stopped only once, to drink from her canteen, and wipe perspiration from her hat band. It was almost mid-afternoon when O'Brien stopped them under the shade of some tall cottonwoods, and built a fire. She gathered some firewood for them, and put a pot of coffee on the fire.

'You could do this all day, couldn't you?' she said as she sat on a fallen log near the fire. Her cheeks were flushed, and her usually neat hair was disheveled.

O'Brien poked at the fire. 'Yes, ma'am. This is right easy work. You'll get used to it. You're doing real well.'

'An hour ago we rode fairly close to a camp of other travelers, and I noticed you made a detour around it. Why were you making an effort to avoid contact?'

He was squatting on his haunches near her, his Stetson tipped low over his face. 'Out here, Sarah, you never know what kind of folks you might run on to. And that's especially true in the Territory, like I told you. We had nothing to gain by making contact, and maybe a lot to lose.'

'You seem a naturally suspicious man.'

O'Brien looked over at her from under the Stetson. 'There ain't nothing natural about it. The trail makes you that way.'

'I hope it doesn't do that to me,' she said.

'I hope it does,' he countered.

Sarah frowned at him, trying to figure him out. 'It seems like you've had a hard life out here, O'Brien. I don't ever see you laugh, or even smile.'

'I wouldn't trade this for nothing,' he told her. 'I'm never more content than when I'm hunkered down in a hardship camp, drinking bad coffee and eating trail grub, and listening to the prairie around me. It's other folks that took the smile off my face, ma'am. Sorry if I ain't good company.'

'I like your company,' she admitted. 'You're not like other men, who are either flirting with me, or finding ways to dislike me because I speak well. You're not judgmental, and you don't hold prejudices.'

He turned and gave her a half-smile. 'You're still talking funny,' he said.

She laughed. 'You're right. I'll try harder. I'll go get that rabbit you shot earlier, and clean it.'

'You sure you're up to it?'

'I'm going to live out here, aren't I? I have to be up to it.'

They skinned and cleaned the rabbit O'Brien had shot, and roasted it over their fire. They still had some biscuits left over from before, and O'Brien opened a tin of beans. It all tasted good to Sarah. There was no stream in the vicinity, so O'Brien cleaned their plates and cups with sand.

'You can only eat rabbit for so long,' he told her as they were packing up again. 'It's too lean – you get protein poisoning.'

She studied his bearded, masculine face. 'You know a lot, Mr Hunter.'

54

'You have to,' he told her. 'If you want to last out here.'

After the horses were watered and their gear packed up, Sarah excused herself to go off into the bushes for a few minutes. There was little privacy on the trail, and she needed it at that moment.

'Here, you can take this Schofield with you,' O'Brien told her.

'I'll be all right,' she said. 'I'll be just over there behind the trees.'

Before he could protest, she walked into cover and he turned to cinch up the Appaloosa's saddle. Then he heard her scream.

He slid his Winchester from its scabbard and hurried into the trees. When he got there, he saw Sarah standing with her riding pants unbuckled, staring down a big bear. It was just thirty feet away.

'O'Brien!' she cried out in a muffled voice.

Seeing O'Brien, the bear rose up on to its hind legs, and towered over them. It opened its mouth and emitted a frightening roar.

'Stand still. He wants us to turn our backs on him and run,' O'Brien said quietly. 'Just do exactly what I tell you.'

'All right,' she said in a tremulous voice.

'Now just take a few steps backward till you're behind me. Very slow,' he told her.

The bear was down again, and growling in its throat: it meant business. It kicked some dirt up, and growled again. Sarah flinched with every move of the bear, but slowly stepped back behind O'Brien.

'OK, that's good,' he said. 'He's focused on me. Now let's both just move back a few more steps.'

But as they started their retreat, the bear roared out again, and started a charge. The Winchester went up. The bear was twenty feet away, then ten.

'Shoot it! Shoot it!' Sarah screamed.

The bear stopped, and reared up a second time. Very close to O'Brien. O'Brien let out a growling roar of his own, right in the bear's face. His rifle was trained on its chest.

The roar from O'Brien startled the bear. It went down again, pawing the ground, kicking dirt up on him, studying his face, and the rifle. Then it turned and ambled off through the trees.

'Oh, mercy! Oh, heavens! What happened?'

'I called his bluff,' O'Brien said, still staring after the bear. It was now out of sight. 'He had run on to men before, and recognized the rifle. And he knew I meant business, just like he did.'

He let the Winchester fall to his side. 'Come on, let's quiet the mounts. They saw the bear, too.' He turned and walked back to the horses, with Sarah staring hard after him.

When they were ready to saddle up, Sarah was finally settling down inside, and had stopped trembling. What amazed her was that O'Brien had treated the incident as if it were just another camp chore.

'I think we can still make Sulphur Creek by dark if we keep at it,' he was saying casually to her, standing beside the Appaloosa 'I'd ordinarily ride right through. But we'll get you a hotel room, so you can get a good rest tonight. You're going to need it.'

She was still staring at him as if he were an alien from Mars. 'I still don't understand. Why didn't you kill the bear?'

O'Brien regarded her curiously, as if she were a child asking obvious questions. 'I looked in his eye. I didn't think he wanted a death fight. We don't need table meat, and the

56

hide didn't look that marketable. Why kill it?'

'Because he might have killed us?'

'I figured that probably wouldn't happen, ma'am,' O'Brien said, frowning slightly. 'Are we going to kick this to death?'

Her face stiffened. 'No. I'm finished. But the next time I go into the bushes, I'll take that Schofield with me. Since I don't mind using it.'

Now O'Brien couldn't suppress a small smile. He was adjusting his saddle, and he turned to face her. 'Oh, that wasn't for bears, Sarah. If you'd shot him with that, he'd have come on in and torn your head off.' He turned away again, and mounted the Appaloosa.

'Well!' she said under her breath. Then she mounted her pinto and followed O'Brien out of their camp.

CHAPTER SIX

Sarah recovered from her anger toward O'Brien within the hour, and soon was glad that he had spared the bear's life. Now she had learned something else about this close-mouthed chaperone of hers: she had presumed that because he had killed up north on that ranch, and because he had been a professional hunter, life would be cheap to him, but it was clear he was reluctant to shoot an animal unless he could make use of it for some utilitarian purpose. Recalling his impatience with that man who had harassed her in Barrow's Corner, and the violence that followed, she concluded that he might have more tolerance toward animals than other men.

They arrived in Sulphur Creek just before dark. It was a bigger town than Barrow's Corner, and had a bigger hotel. It also had three stores, a fancy bank, and a clapboard opera house that was boarded over. There was even a small restaurant on the main street, and after O'Brien had registered them at the hotel and obtained adjoining rooms, and had taken their mounts down to a small hostelry for the night, they walked down to the restaurant for an evening meal.

O'Brien had been in Sulphur Creek years ago, and had bad memories from there. It had always been a rough town, and now it looked about the same. There were a few ranches in the area, and that drew in cowboys to blow off steam, whom O'Brien tried to avoid like the plague. That night they were riding up and down the main street shooting off their six-shooters and acting wild. So, as usual, O'Brien had carried his Winchester into the restaurant with them and laid it on a chair beside him. The waiter eyed it with diffidence, and spoke to O'Brien about it.

'You aren't supposed to bring any long guns in here. It's against our policy.'

They had already ordered. 'Just bring our food, and make it edible,' O'Brien said without looking up.

When the man left, Sarah turned to him. 'You were very rude to him. I wondered why you brought the gun in. This seems like a civilized place.'

'It probably is,' he said. A married couple sat over in a corner and watched O'Brien warily.

Sarah shook her pretty head. 'My goodness. You are different.'

Their meal came shortly. It was steak for O'Brien and a chicken breast for Sarah. The meal was well cooked, and O'Brien enjoyed it. When they were almost finished, two cowboys came in and sat down at a table not far away. They looked over at O'Brien, and the Winchester, and then exchanged some low talk.

'Those men keep looking at you,' Sarah said to him. 'Maybe we ought to leave.'

'They come in from a ranch,' he told her. 'Just drink your coffee.'

She sipped at her coffee, but kept an eye on the other men. The married couple paid their bill of fare and left. The cowboys ordered coffee and nothing else. Finally, one of them called over to O'Brien.

'Hey, mister! That your Winchester?'

O'Brien looked over at them, but said nothing.

'Maybe you ought to answer him,' Sarah said, looking tense.

'They're just entertaining themselves,' he said. 'No need.'

'You really know how to shoot that thing? Wearing them rawhides don't make you no hunter, you know.'

There was a lot of low laughter then between them. Sarah was getting nervous. 'We'd better return to the hotel. We're finished, anyway.'

'You go on,' O'Brien told her. 'I'll just finish my coffee, and see you back there.'

'Go with me,' she urged him.

He looked over at her. 'You go on now.'

She hesitated, then got up and left, looking over her shoulder at the two cowboys. In a moment she was out on the street and gone.

'That your wife, hunter?' the second ranch-hand called over. He was slim and bony-looking, and had pockmarks on his lower face. His companion, who had called out first, was heavier, and had a purple birthmark on his left cheek. They were both carrying sidearms, and they were obviously looking for trouble.

'She looked good enough to spend some time with,' the heavy one grinned. 'I guess she does most of the shooting out there, huh? And you just carry that Winchester around to give the right impression.'

O'Brien sipped at his coffee; it was almost gone. 'Why don't you boys give it up?' he said without looking up. 'You ain't all that funny.'

The slim one gave his companion a sober look. 'The hunter can talk after all. So we ain't funny enough for you, heh? Well, when Gus here tells a joke, he expects you to laugh. You ain't laughing, hunter?'

'That's right,' Gus said. 'We think it would be nice if you laughed, trail bum.' He rose and walked over to O'Brien's table. O'Brien put his right hand on his rifle. Gus stood over him threateningly. 'Well?'

O'Brien looked up at him. 'You're as ugly a man as I seen in a long time, Gus. Is that why you make a fool of yourself like this?'

Gus's face flushed, and his companion got up and came over beside him. 'What did he say to you?'

'He said I'm ugly,' Gus said in a low, deadly voice. He drew the revolver on his hip. 'Now, you prairie snake, let's see how ugly you are with a hole in your forehead!' He aimed the revolver at O'Brien's head, breathlessly, and his finger whitened over the trigger.

O'Brien swung the Winchester's barrel in a wide arc toward Gus's legs, and it cracked loudly there against his kneecaps, fracturing the right one. Gus fell to the floor, his gun firing explosively and just missing O'Brien's left ear. He lost his gun, and was yelling in pain. The companion then drew on O'Brien, but O'Brien turned the Winchester on him before he could clear leather.

'Go ahead,' O'Brien said casually. 'I'll put three in you before you can get a second shot in.'

Gus was still yelling on the floor between them. The slim man stared at the muzzle of the rifle, and then down at his companion. He still held his revolver in his hand, but it was not aimed at O'Brien. 'You broke his kneecap. I heard it snap.'

O'Brien got up, swung the barrel of the rifle again, and it smacked up against the side of the other man's face, cracking bone in his cheek. He went staggering backwards

61

under the impact, firing off his revolver into the floor, chipping up wood as he went, and falling against the table they had occupied, taking it down with him. He was stunned, his jaw working. O'Brien walked over and kicked his gun out of his grasp.

'You better keep them guns holstered for a while,' O'Brien growled down at them. They were both lying awkwardly on the floor, grimacing in pain. 'You don't seem to have the know-how for stuff like this.'

He turned then and threw some coins on his table for the meals, and then quietly left the restaurant. The waiter, who had watched the whole thing at a safe distance, whistled between his teeth.

'I never seen the like,' he muttered to himself, staring hard at the two injured cowhands. 'Never in my born days did I see anything quite like that.'

The two ranch-hands were taken to a local doctor that night to have broken bones tended, and didn't get back to their ranch till the following morning, long after O'Brien and Sarah were gone. O'Brien got Sarah up at just before dawn again, and they set out with just coffee for breakfast. O'Brien wanted to get to Fort Revenge as quickly as possible, to get Sarah off his hands.

After they had been riding for about an hour, Sarah guided her pinto up beside O'Brien's Appaloosa. 'I heard the desk clerk talking this morning with one of the locals,' she said.

He glanced over at her. 'What about it?'

'They were saying that two ranch-hands were badly injured last night, at the restaurant where we had supper. Were those the two who were bothering us?'

He sighed, staring out over the plains, watching for

trouble. 'Yep. The same ones.'

'And you were the one who hurt them?'

'I just busted them up a little, ma'am.'

'Why would you do that, O'Brien? Why do you have to take everything to the extreme?'

He stared over at her for a long moment. This was becoming tiresome, trying to explain everything that happened out here to this female greenhorn. 'I didn't take nothing to the extreme, Sarah,' he said curtly. 'The extreme would of been to take them both down. Permanent.'

'Just because they were making jokes about us?' she said. 'That seems pretty extreme to me, O'Brien. It makes me uncomfortable to travel with a man who uses physical violence to settle matters.'

He wondered if it was worthwhile to explain that they were about to kill him. He reined his mount in, and Sarah did likewise. He turned to face her, making his saddle squeak under his weight.

'Well, I'm what you got, Sarah. You can't ride this trail alone. It's only a couple more days till we reach Fort Revenge. Just try to put up with me till then, and you won't never have to bother with me again. If I see you on the street in town, you can just look the other way. Does that suit you?'

She was surprised at the remarks. O'Brien seemed so downright intractable sometimes. He never apologized, never tried to explain his behavior. If you didn't understand him, he just didn't care. She had never met a man just like him.

'I don't want that,' she said to him, subdued now. 'I hope we do see each other after we arrive. I'd want you to meet my new husband, after I'm married. If you wouldn't find some reason to knock him down.'

O'Brien shook his head, and spurred his mount ahead, and she followed. 'It's probably too soon to try to explain any of this to you. But I'll tell you this. Hunters and mountain men are a breed apart, and town folk and cowboys know that, and don't like it. It don't pay to be different out here, any more than it does in Boston. It attracts trouble to you, whether you want it or not.'

Sarah turned and studied his square, rugged face, and was surprised at the depth of his explanation. She had not thought him capable of such insight into human nature. 'I understand, O'Brien. I had some of that myself, after I reached a certain age unmarried. My old school friends began to ignore me, and men shied away.'

'I can't imagine that,' he observed. 'I mean, men not noticing a pretty woman like yourself.'

She blushed a little, and remembered why she liked him. He was capable of little kindnesses, despite his rough demeanor.

'That's very kind,' she managed.

'No, ma'am. Just an observation.'

They stopped only briefly at noon, and then rode hard all the rest of that day, so that Fort Revenge could be reached at the end of the following day. Sarah was very sore when they camped that evening with about two hours of light left in the sky. There was a drizzle of rain as they were setting up camp, but it stopped in time for them to build a fire and have an evening meal.

They were just cleaning up from the meal, and O'Brien was over watering the horses from a nearby creek, when he looked up and scented the air. Sarah, who was washing their utensils, took no notice. O'Brien listened for a moment but heard nothing. It was almost dark, and past a time when a rifle would be needed for a long-distance shot, so he went to Sarah's horse and took the Schofield revolver off its irons and stuck it in the back of his belt. Sarah was still busy cleaning up, so he hadn't alarmed her. By the time he came back over to the fire, though, he heard the soft hoofbeats of three horses.

'Sarah. We're going to have company,' he said easily to her.

'What?'

'Go and sit down on that stump there on the far side of the fire. Do what I tell you now. And don't speak, or yell out. You understand?'

Sarah swallowed back her sudden fear. 'All right.' She went and sat on the stump just as the three riders appeared from behind a clump of low trees. They were Pawnee.

'Oh, no!' she whispered. 'It's them again!'

'It probably ain't the same ones,' he said. 'Now, remember what I told you.'

The Indians came riding slowly into camp, and unlike the ones who had attacked Sarah's wagon, these were armed with old Army rifles. They came right into the light and looked down on the two travelers haughtily.

O'Brien felt the weight of the Schofield behind him and was glad he had gone to get it while there was time. He nodded to the Indians.

'Welcome to our camp,' he said in Pawnee.

They stared at him, looking Sarah over.

'You can share our coffee,' O'Brien added. He held a cup out to the riders.

The Pawnee nearest them was a well-muscled, lean fellow wearing buskskins and moccasins. He dismounted with his rifle and walked over to O'Brien. Very confident. Very sure of himself. He took the cup of coffee and drank it down in one long gulp, then threw the cup on to the ground.

Watching O'Brien's face to see his reaction. O'Brien was impassive.

'I hope Two Eagles is well,' he finally said, ignoring the insult. He had met the Pawnee chief from the Territory reservation years ago.

The Pawnee frowned. 'Why do you use the name of Two Eagles?'

'I know him well,' O'Brien responded. 'Does he know you're out here on the Fort Revenge trail tonight?'

The frown deepened. 'We go where we please. We do not recognize the white man's tribal prisons!'

O'Brien nodded. 'I don't, either. Take my good wishes to Two Eagles, and let us pass in peace.'

The Pawnees still on horseback held their rifles at the ready, seeming to be hoping to use them. The one on the ground jerked a finger toward Sarah. 'You have a woman with you. Does she belong to you?'

O'Brien hesitated. 'No,' he said. 'But she is spoken for.'

'I like her hair,' the Pawnee told him.

'What's he saying?' Sarah said nervously from behind him.

'I told you not to speak,' O'Brien said carefully. The Pawnees had all looked over at her.

'You are in Pawnee country,' the one facing him said now. 'Our tribal custom demands tribute. You must pay us.'

O'Brien had expected this. 'We don't have much. You can have our ration of corn flour, and some chicory.'

'We do not need corn flour,' the Pawnee told him. 'We have lost squaws to the white man's coughing sickness. We will take the woman. You can get another one in Fort Revenge.'

He walked over to Sarah, and she gasped out as he looked her over. O'Brien drew the Schofield from behind

66

his back and leveled it at the Pawnee. The ones on horse-back quickly raised their rifles, ready to fire. But O'Brien's revolver was aimed at their comrade's head.

'You can't have the woman,' he said in a level voice.

The Pawnee confronting Sarah turned arrogantly to him, and eyed the Schofield contemptuously. 'You will not stop us, hunter.'

'Maybe. But when you meet your ancestors shortly, be sure to tell them that this buffalo hunter gave it his best try.'

The Pawnee's face changed, and he studied O'Brien more closely. 'Are you the one who hunted buffalo with the Cheyenne? Two Eagles has spoken of such a man.'

'That's right,' O'Brien said. 'I hunted them everywhere.' His revolver was still aimed at the Pawnee's head.

The Pawnee turned to his companions. 'This is the bear-man of the Lakota.'

They exchanged a dark look, and one of them muttered something. The one near Sarah came over to O'Brien, and looked him over carefully. 'I believe you are him,' he said after a moment. His rifle was still hanging loose at his side. 'Two Eagles says you are a great hunter. If we kill you, he will be displeased.'

'I'm glad to hear that,' O'Brien told him.

'We will not take the woman,' the Pawnee said. 'But do not bring her through here again. We will take your chicory. All of it.'

O'Brien nodded, and stuck the revolver into his belt. 'That's fair.'

He went to the Appaloosa's saddle-bag, took the big sack of chicory out, and handed it over to the Indian. The Pawnee looked it over, hefted it, and nodded. He looked into O'Brien's eyes. 'You may go in peace, Lakota man.'

O'Brien nodded. 'Tell Two Eagles I wish him well.'

A moment later the Pawnee was mounted again, and the three rode off into the night. Sarah let out a long, shaky breath and put her head between her knees. O'Brien went over to her, and knelt beside her.

'Are you OK?'

She looked up at him. 'I'll be all right. They were going to take me, weren't they?'

'They had that notion, all right.'

'What did you do? They just rode away when you gave them that bag of chicory.'

O'Brien shrugged. 'They wasn't really bad men. When they found out I knew their chief, they was pretty nice.'

'But you had to draw the revolver. And then you said something to him that seemed to make him change his mind.'

'It was just palaver, ma'am.' He stood back up. 'There's still some coffee in the pot. Maybe you could use a good swig.'

Sarah rose, too, and felt a little unsteady. 'Yes, thanks. I think I could.' She came over to the fire, and O'Brien poured her a cup of the hot coffee, and she sipped at it, trying to calm herself.

'We won't have no more trouble from them now,' O'Brien assured her. 'And by tomorrow noon we should be in Fort Revenge.'

Sarah looked at him over her cup. 'That just might be my happiest day since I left Boston,' she said ruefully.

O'Brien nodded. 'I hope it is, Sarah,' he told her. 'I really hope it is.'

CHAPTER SEVEN

That same evening, Emmet Purcell's foreman Corey McGraw and ranch-hand Wade Lucas arrived in Sulphur Creek, just a day's ride behind O'Brien and Sarah Carter.

Lucas was disgruntled by McGraw's persistence in hunting O'Brien, and having no luck. They had asked about O'Brien in Barrow's Corner, at the hotel, but O'Brien had only registered Sarah, and they didn't know her name. There was also a different desk clerk on duty now, who hadn't met either Sarah or O'Brien. Now, in Sulphur Creek, they hitched their mounts outside the same restaurant where O'Brien and Sarah had had an evening meal, and O'Brien had had to deal with the two cowpunchers. They were going to go to the hotel after they had eaten, and inquire there, but had no intention of asking at the restaurant. When they got seated, the same waiter who had served O'Brien and Sarah came over to them.

'What can I get you, boys?' he asked them.

They both ordered steak and fries, and McGraw noted that there were no other customers. 'Is it always this quiet in here? The locals ain't avoiding your food, are they?'

'Oh, you're a little early,' the waiter said. 'We usually get a small crowd. If you think it's quiet, you should have been here last night. There was a real ruckus. Had to take a couple boys down to the doctor.'

Lucas looked up at him. 'Yeah? What happened?'

'Oh, this big hunter come in. With a woman, but she left. There was some talk between this hunter and a couple of ranch-hands, and he roughed them up real good.'

Lucas and McGraw exchanged a look, and McGraw turned to the waiter. 'You say this big man was a hunter?'

'Well, I reckon he was. He was wearing them rawhides, and carrying a rifle with him. I told him we don't allow no big guns in here, but he didn't pay no attention. He was as ornery as they come.'

'Did he wear a beard?' McGraw asked.

'Why, yes, he did,' the waiter said. 'Do you know him?'

McGraw looked over at Lucas. 'It's him.'

'I don't mean to throw mud on nobody,' the waiter said, 'but I hope he ain't no friend of yours. You wouldn't be welcome in town if he was.'

'He's no friend of ours,' McGraw told him. 'Did you hear him and the woman talking?'

The waiter pursed his lips. 'They mentioned Fort Revenge. I think they were headed there together.'

McGraw got a look of smug satisfaction on his square face. 'Well, well. You see how it pays to keep at it?' To Lucas: 'Looks like we found him.'

Lucas wasn't as pleased about it. Now they had to try to kill a man who might not be that easy to kill, and who had nothing to do with rustling Purcell's cattle. 'Yeah,' he said quietly. 'Looks like we did.'

'Well, I'll get them steaks fried up for you,' the waiter said, and he left their table and disappeared into the kitchen.

'We ought to send a wire off to Emmet,' Lucas suggested.

'To let him know what's happening. He'll be real pleased to hear we're closing in.'

'No, no,' McGraw said firmly. 'What if something goes wrong then? After telling Emmet we think it's a done deal? No, we'll report back after the fact, when this O'Brien is pushing up daisies in some Fort Revenge cemetery.'

Lucas arched his heavy brow. 'OK, Corey. You're making the decisions here.'

'If we get up early tomorrow, we can be in Fort Revenge not long after their arrival there. And we won't make this no face-down. He didn't give Tully no fair chance. Why should we give him one? We'll find him some place where he least expects trouble, and just back-shoot him. That's the only sure way. We'll both unload into him, and then ride out of there. I hear there's no law there, anyway, so it ought to be easy.'

'Yeah,' Lucas said doubtfully. 'Easy.'

It rained off and on during the night. Out on the trail partway to Fort Revenge, O'Brien and Sarah had to hunker under a mesquite tree and hold blankets over their heads. They got little sleep. But they were only a half-day's ride out now, and expected to reach their destination at or before noon of that next day.

When morning came, the sky was still overcast but the rain had stopped. It was the same on the trail from Fort Revenge to Stillwater, where Lem Foley was returning to Fort Revenge after picking up a small payroll from a bank in Stillwater, and three passengers. He had had a good trip so far, missing the early rain, and making good time on wet roads.

At a point two hours out of Fort Revenge, where he passed under high rocks, suddenly four riders came out of

71

nowhere, firing off their guns, and stopped his coach. The four-horse team reared and guffered at all the commotion as Foley tried to keep them reined in.

The men were masked, but Foley thought he recognized Ben Driscoll's voice when the coach was ordered to stop. The passengers, two ranchers and a young woman, leaned out of the windows to see what was happening, and quickly understood the situation.

'Oh, dear!' the woman was crying out. 'Oh, no!'

Foley was now surrounded by Ben Driscoll and his cohorts, all of them wearing bandannas around their faces, and long coats. They were all still mounted.

'Don't shoot!' Foley yelled out. 'We'll cooperate! You can have what we got!'

One-Eye Wylie moved his horse up close to Foley, aimed his Webley RIC .45 at Foley's head, and squeezed the trigger, hitting Foley in the left eye and blowing a hole in the back of his head. Foley's head whiplashed, and then he fell sidewise off the seat, tumbling to the ground at Wylie's horse's feet. The young woman screamed loudly.

'Get the cash box,' Driscoll said to Latimer, on the far side of the coach. 'It should be under the seat up there.'

Latimer nodded, dismounted, and climbed up on to the seat and raised a lid. Then he was handing a heavy box down to Maynard Quinn. They secured it on to Quinn's mount, which was a big, strapping quarter horse. Driscoll also dismounted, and called in to the passengers.

'All right! Everybody out!'

Wylie remained mounted, and Quinn re-mounted as the passengers tumbled out of the coach: two scared ranchers and a pale-faced woman dressed in finery.

'Don't kill us,' the older rancher blurted out. 'You can have what we've got.'

'Get over here,' Driscoll said to Latimer.

Jake Latimer approached the passengers with a cloth bag. 'OK, all of you. Dump your wallets, cash, and jewelry into this.'

It took them several minutes to follow his order. Wylie and Quinn sat on their mounts, guns trained on the passengers; Driscoll watched the whole thing closely, behind his bandanna. After a few minutes, Latimer turned to him.

'OK. I think we got it all.'

Driscoll nodded. He walked over in front of the nearest rancher, the younger of the two. 'I'm in a good mood today. I'm letting you all go on your way. You can drive the coach, mister. But if any of you tries to cause us trouble in Stillwater or Fort Revenge, we won't be so nice the next time we run into you.'

'We won't say anything,' the older rancher said.

'Just let us go, please,' the woman said, in a tremulous voice.

'Where you headed, honey?' Wylie called down to her. 'You and me could ride my horse.' In Wylie's case, his bandanna was pulled up over his entire face, with narrow eye-holes cut in, to hide his bad eye, which could have been recalled later for identification.

Driscoll gave him a burning look from behind his neckerchief. 'Get back inside, you two.' He pointed at the younger rancher. 'You. Get up on the box. And whip that team hard.'

A few minutes later the stagecoach drove away in a small cloud of dust, and as it passed out of sight, Driscoll pulled his bandanna down and grinned.

'Well, what did I tell you, boys? Did we make a haul? Just the loot from the passengers would be enough. But we got the payroll box, too.'

73

'I hope there's gold in there,' Wylie grumbled, pulling the mask off and revealing the scarred eye. 'I hate paper money.'

'It felt heavy,' Latimer offered. 'There must be metal in there.'

'Why don't we find out?' Quinn suggested. 'Right here.'

'I told you,' Driscoll said. 'We open it up at my place. Somebody else might come along any minute. Come on, let's ride. We got Christmas waiting for us back there.'

He stepped over the dead body of Lem Foley without even looking down at it. Then he and Latimer mounted up and they all rode off into the high rocks again, to take a circuitous route back to Fort Revenge.

They had had a successful day, and Driscoll was planning for more.

Smith's assaulted coach arrived in Fort Revenge at 10.57 a.m. according to his old railroad watch, and when he saw the rancher driving the team, he knew immediately what had happened. The female passenger's face was tear-streaked, and the two men talked so fast it was difficult to figure out exactly how it had all developed. Smith couldn't believe that Foley was dead; he was the first driver he had hired for his new company. And the lost payroll would cause him trouble with the Stillwater bank, and with local ranchers.

Less than an hour after that arrival, Driscoll and his small gang were back at his old shack, and when they opened the cash box, they found stacks of silver dollars, a few gold double eagles, and some legal papers. With the loot from the coach passengers, it was a good first haul. But Wylie was dissatisfied with the gold, and wanted to go again in a day or two. Driscoll, though, knew that it was prudent to wait a week or two now, to let things cool off. Quinn figured his share would help save his restaurant, and Latimer would just add it to his profits from selling off his livestock and acreage, and let him lead the indolent life he had planned for himself. He had now given up on Sarah's coming, and impatiently decided he might lure a local girl to his place to keep house for him.

At a half-hour past noon, O'Brien and Sarah rode into town.

O'Brien sought out Shanghai Smith's Territorial Express first, and found Smith out on the porch of his headquarters, speaking with another driver named R.C. Funk and the part-time mayor of the town, one Avery Spencer. Smith had just instructed Funk to ride out and bring Foley's body back for burial, and Spencer was there to talk about the lost payroll. When Smith heard O'Brien and Sarah ride up and stop, he turned with a furrowed brow, but then his pudgy face lit up as it hadn't in days.

'Well, I'll be a puffed-up horny toad! O'Brien?'

O'Brien sat heavily on his mount. 'The same,' he said. He dismounted, and helped Sarah off her pinto as Smith was making further exclamations.

Smith came at him like a freight train, and threw his bear-like arms around O'Brien, catching him off-guard and almost knocking him down. 'It's really you, you old tatonka bull! You got my letter!' In a booming voice that almost made O'Brien's ears ring.

O'Brien frowned heavily, and shoved Smith off him. 'What's the matter with you, you overstuffed cougar bait? You're making me skittery as a turkey in a wire pen.'

Smith was still grinning ear to ear. 'If you ain't a sight for sore eyes! How long has it been, partner? Five years? Six?'

'Four,' O'Brien corrected him. 'And it seems like two. My ears are still red from that voice of yours. And you still smell

75

like buffalo dung.'

Smith burst out in such uproarious laughter that Sarah stepped back a step. 'You old bullfrog!' Smith exclaimed loudly. 'Hey! Who you riding with there? Did you get some sense and find yourself a woman?'

Both O'Brien and Sarah were embarrassed by that question. She stepped forward again. 'I'm promised to one of your local farmers,' she said quietly. 'I've come from Boston to marry him.'

Smith's ruddy, fat-crowded face showed curiosity. 'How about that!'

'This is Sarah Carter,' O'Brien told him.

Smith nodded. 'Pleasured to meet up with you, ma'am. I'm Shanghai Smith, I run this stageline. This here is our mayor, Avery Spencer, and my driver, R.C.'

'Welcome to Fort Revenge, Miss Carter,' Spencer told her. He had thin, graying hair and a pot belly, and was a local rancher. 'Good to see a young woman come to live with us. Who did you come to marry?'

'His name is Jake Latimer,' Sarah said. 'I understand he owns a nice little farm outside of town here.'

'Oh,' Smith said, his heavy face sobering.

'Jake Latimer wants a wife?' the driver Funk said in surprise.

But the mayor stepped in quickly. 'Well, of course he does,' he said with a bright smile. 'He must get pretty lonesome out there all by hisself. That was pretty smart of him, come to think of it. To send off for a bride. Why, I'd do it myself if I could afford it.'

They all just looked at him. O'Brien took Sarah's arm and brought her up on to the porch with him. 'You got a place where the lady can freshen up, Smitty, before she rides out to the farm?'

'Oh, sure,' Smith said. 'Come on inside, ma'am. Talk to you later, Mr Mayor. Funk, you head on out to find Foley.'

The three of them went inside then, and O'Brien looked around. They were in a large room, with two desks in it, and lots of papers on the desks. On the wall there was a long row of file cabinets, some of the drawers open. In the corner was a wood stove with a pot of coffee sitting on it. Out in back there was another long room with double bunks, and a washroom. Sarah was shown to the washroom, and cleaned up there while O'Brien and Smith recalled old times together. When she re-emerged, hair combed neatly and face freshened, Smith had finished telling O'Brien about the hold-up.

'How about that December morning in Montana when we come on that herd standing in deep snow?' Smith was booming. 'It made the snow black as far as the eye could see. It took us all morning to work that herd. You was bucked off your mount and almost trampled to death!' He shook his head. 'You should have died fifty times over out there. Me, too. I don't know how we come through it. Oh, there's the lady! Looking like she stepped out of the Sears-Roebuck catalogue!'

O'Brien looked up from a cup of coffee he was drinking, and studied Sarah for the first time in days. She was a handsome woman, no doubt of it. He hoped Latimer was worthy of her.

'I'm ready to ride out to the Latimer farm, O'Brien. If you have the directions now.' She was very nervous about meeting Latimer. 'I won't be staying there tonight, of course. Is there a hotel here, Mr Smith?'

'No, ma'am. But there's a Mrs Barstow rents out rooms to my passengers that are going on through. I expect she can find you a bed.'

'I'll see her later,' she agreed.

O'Brien rose from his chair. 'Well, Sarah. Let's go meet your future husband.'

'Jake might take some getting used to,' Smith said as they walked to the door. 'Remember, ma'am, he's been living alone.' At this point, he was already wondering if Ben Driscoll and his cohort Wylie had anything to do with the stage robbery, and remembering that Latimer had been seen hanging around with them in the recent past.

'I understand, Mr Smith,' Sarah said. But she was very tight inside.

O'Brien had already promised Sarah to deliver her personally to her expected groom, so they rode out to the Latimer farm together. Sarah was very quiet on the way there, and O'Brien kept looking over at her to see if she was all right. It was obvious that she was very tense about this meeting.

'I reckon these mail-order marriages are always a mite nerve-stretching,' he suggested to her as they rode up to the old farmhouse. 'It will be OK, Sarah.'

'Are you going to be in town for a while?' she asked.

'Oh, sure. Smitty and me got some catching up to do. And he tells me there's good hunting and trapping hereabouts. That will keep me in and out of town a lot. I reckon you and me will meet up regular-like.'

'I hope so,' she admitted. 'Well. Here we are.'

They dismounted before an unpainted, two-story house with a broken bannister railing and overgrown ivy, and hitched their mounts to a rail there. O'Brien frowned slightly at the appearance of the place, but said nothing.

'Hallo inside!' he called out.

A moment later Latimer appeared at the front door, and came out on to the porch. His shirt was unbuttoned halfway down his chest, and his hair was uncombed. 'Who is it?' he said caustically to them.

'I'm O'Brien. And this here is Sarah Carter. Are you Jake Latimer?'

Latimer nodded absently. 'Wait a minute! You're Sarah? From Boston?'

She was looking him over soberly. 'Yes, Jake. I'm Sarah.'

He came down off the porch grinning. 'I'd given up on you! Just look at this!' He grabbed her unexpectedly, and hugged her tightly to him, scaring her a little, and then tried to kiss her on her lips.

Sarah struggled in his grasp, and then pushed him away. 'Wait, Jake. Not so fast. We're not married yet.'

O'Brien was surprised at the show of intimacy, but kept his silence.

'Oh, sure, that's right,' Latimer was saying. He had been given his share of the robbery loot, and was very pleased with his new life. 'Say, who's this with you?'

'I found Sarah out on the trail,' O'Brien told him. 'She needed somebody to ride with.'

Latimer came over boldly and looked O'Brien over. He was almost as tall as the hunter, but not nearly as broad or hard-looking. 'I see. Well, I guess you must have took good care of her, O'Brien.' He pushed his dark hair off his forehead, and they both assessed his good looks. 'Hey. Both of you. Come on in and take a look at the house. I can make coffee.'

O'Brien accepted the invitation, and Sarah was relieved he had. They climbed to the porch over rickety steps and entered a large living room. It was a comfortable-looking place, with overstuffed furniture and prints of old paintings on the walls, left by a previous owner. On a small table centrally lay a gunbelt and holster, holding a Colt .44. Latimer quickly grabbed it and hid it in a sideboard.

'Well. What do you think, Sarah? This will all be yours after we tie the old knot! I sold off some livestock, but we got some chickens out back for eggs, and a milk cow. There's a right nice range in the kitchen for cooking, and a big, soft bed upstairs for a pretty bride!' A wide grin.

Sarah blushed a little. Latimer got them all a cup of tepid coffee, and they all sat around the living room appraising each other. 'I thought you wasn't coming,' Latimer finally continued. 'But the mayor can marry us right away. Tomorrow morning if you want to.'

'Maybe we ought to take a few days to get to know each other,' she suggested.

He arched his brows. 'Well, sure. We can sleep separate till then if that pleases you. I got a second bed upstairs, in another room.'

'I've decided to take a room at Mrs Barstow's place until the wedding,' Sarah told him.

He frowned. 'Hey, now. No need for anything like that. No, sir, you just stay right here with me, little lady. You can cook my meals while you're here. And get this place cleaned up a little bit.'

Sarah glanced over at O'Brien. 'I'd really rather stay at Mrs Barstow's,' she insisted quietly.

Latimer's frown deepened. 'Maybe I didn't make myself clear, Sarah. I don't want you running off to town already when you got a bed right here. I'd be the laughing stock. No, you're commited to me now. This is your place, right here on this farm.'

'You made yourself real clear, all right,' O'Brien interposed then. 'You just ain't listening to the lady. She intends to stay in town till the wedding.'

Latimer narrowed his dark eyes on O'Brien. 'Say, what is

this, anyway? What's been going on with you two, out on the trail alone together?'

O'Brien started to get off his chair, but Sarah stopped him with her eyes. 'Nothing has gone on between us,' she said defensively. She was suddenly angry inside. 'Except friendship. O'Brien saved my life out there, Jake. I wouldn't be here if he hadn't come along.'

Latimer eyed O'Brien darkly. 'Are you staying at Barstow's place too?'

O'Brien shook his head. 'I probably won't even be here tonight. I promised Sarah I'd take her out here to meet you. That's it.'

'Then why don't you leave this alone?' Latimer said evenly, grinning past the harsh words.

O'Brien was trying very hard to hold his temper. If this wasn't the man Sarah expected to marry, he wouldn't have been so tolerant of his behavior. 'I think that's up to Sarah,' he said.

Sarah rose, and so did O'Brien. 'Let's not start off on the wrong foot, Jake. I'll be at Mrs Barstow's tomorrow if you want to visit me there. Maybe we could have a meal there together. Find out about each other. Isn't that a good idea?'

Latimer rose, too, and shot a hard look at O'Brien. 'Well. I'm going to look like a fool. But I reckon I can go along with this a couple of days. After that, if you're not ready to do this, you better get ready. I got a contract.'

Sarah was surprised at his manner. 'I'm sure we'll work it all out,' she said, but was beginning to doubt it. The trouble was, Latimer was her only anchor in town. If she didn't have him, she had nothing. And this whole enterprise, with all its hardships and dangers, was for nothing. 'You know where I'll be tomorrow, if you care to see me.'

Latimer nodded, sober-faced. 'Right. Mrs Barstow's.'

Sarah and O'Brien left then, and as they mounted up and rode away, O'Brien couldn't help wondering if Sarah shouldn't have stayed in Boston, reading her books and attending band concerts on Sunday afternoons. It was true there would have been some boredom in that life back there. But boredom might seem pretty nice compared to what she had ahead of her.

He hoped it would be a whole lot better than it looked at that moment.

After settling Sarah in at Mrs Barstow's, where Sarah was given a pleasant upstairs room with a sunny window, O'Brien left her there, assuring her he wouldn't leave town without saying goodbye. Then he rode down the street to Shanghai Smith's place. Smith was glad to see him back, and invited O'Brien inside for a hot cup of coffee. They sat at Smith's desk, which was piled with papers.

'That was a nice lady you brought with you. I hoped she was yours,' Smith told him. He was bare-headed, and his thinning hair was gray-streaked. He ran a hand through his grizzled beard. 'But I guess you're still pretty much a loner, ain't you, partner?'

'Women always seem a little scared of me,' O'Brien commented. Even with the gray in his hair and beard, he looked very physically capable sitting there, very imposing. He still had no belly and no fat on him. Underneath the rawhides were multiple scars and healed bones from his rough life in the open. 'I reckon it's the beard, and the rawhides.'

'It ain't the beard,' Smith said. 'You just never learned how to talk to people, especially women. You got that manner about you. I'm used to it, but it can put other folks off. You can't help it, the trail made you that way.'

O'Brien gave him a sour look. 'Anything else, Doctor?'

'There. That's what I mean.' Shaking his head. 'Oh, I meant to ask. How did Miss Carter take to Latimer?'

'I reckon it's a mite early to tell,' O'Brien said pensively. 'But I didn't like him at all. I expected better for her.'

Smith stared at his desk top. 'That hold-up we just had out on the Stillwater road. My driver was murdered in cold blood. And I got a pretty good idea who might of done it.'

'Did you send for the federal marshal?'

'What for? I ain't got no real evidence. But this fellow Ben Driscoll was paying a lot of attention to our schedules without ever buying a ticket. And he hangs out with a known outlaw, a man called One-Eye Wylie. There was four of them that robbed the stage, so if it was them, they had help. They're in Maynard Quinn's restaurant all the time, and they been seen out at Latimer's farm, too.'

O'Brien frowned. 'Are you sure?'

Smith was busting out of his clothes behind a leather vest. His fat-crowded face looked particularly ruddy-pink at that moment. 'It's only what I hear. Latimer could be as innocent as me. At least he wants a woman to make a life with, and that speaks well for him. I don't think we could take any of this to Miss Carter.'

O'Brien sat there thinking about that. 'I didn't take him for no preacher. But if you're wrong about him, we could ruin his marriage.'

'That's my thinking on it.'

O'Brien put his coffee cup down on Smith's desk. 'Well, I hope you don't have no more trouble with this, Smitty. You deserve some good luck. Now, you mentioned some good trapping around here in your letter. You going to ride out with me and put my nose in it?'

Smith blew his fat cheeks out. 'I been meaning to talk to you about that. Since I wrote that letter, the Paiute have about cleaned this area out, O'Brien. The reservations ain't that far from here, you know. We even had Pawnee harassing travelers.'

O'Brien was stoic. 'So you're telling me I rode clear down here for nothing.'

'Oh, I reckon there's some fur to be had out there. But I don't know if you could make a living at it now. I'm right sorry about that letter. The one time I take pen to paper in years, I set you out on a wild goose chase.'

O'Brien shook his shaggy head. 'Don't pay it no mind. I'll travel on south, away from the reservations. Some of that country is still pretty wild. There might be some good trapping left down there.'

'Well, that brings me to something else,' Smith went on, taking a deep breath in. 'There'a a couple of jobs open here.'

O'Brien frowned. 'Jobs?'

'I need another driver. Actually, more than that. It pays pretty good, and I remember you used to drive for the hide companies. What do you think?'

O'Brien deepened the frown. 'Me, drive a stage? I don't think so, Smitty. I don't know nothing but hunting and trapping now. But I appreciate the offer.'

Smith sighed. 'All right, then. Let's talk about the other job. Mayor Spencer wants to hire a town marshal. Just on a temporary basis, till we figure out if we're going to have more trouble on the stagelines.'

'Do I look like a gunslinger?' O'Brien said caustically.

'Just hear me out. I happen to know you done this once before, on a temporary basis, to help out a friend. And Spencer knows about your expertise with guns.'

'How would he know that?' O'Brien asked pointedly.

Smith shrugged sheepishly. I might have mentioned it, I guess. But that's not the point. You'd be perfect for the job.

Spencer told me he'd pay twice the usual salary, and it would be just for one month. While this emergency exists.'

O'Brien stared down at his boots. 'That is good money, and I'm about broke. But I guess I'll pass.'

'You could use the money to finance a trip south to look for good trapping grounds,' Smith cajoled him. 'And last of all, if you help us stop these hold-ups, you might just save my company, partner.'

O'Brien gave him a knowing look, and sat forward on his chair. His bank account in Kansas City was about depleted, and he had little cash on him now. 'Can you put me up for a couple nights?'

Smith nodded quickly. 'Absolutely. I got several unoccupied bunks in the back room. You'd have to sleep with snoring drivers, but I got blankets and a wash room back there.'

O'Brien hesitated, then rose. 'I won't leave today. I'll give all of this some thought.' He was also thinking of Sarah's uncertain situation. 'I'll let you know, Smitty.'

Smith was grinning widely. 'I'll get a bunk ready for you.'

'And I'll get the Appaloosa bedded down at the hostelry.' He rose and settled his Stetson on to his wild-looking hair.

Smith was up from his desk, too, and stomped around to O'Brien, making the floor shake. 'Supper is on me, partner. Steaks at Quinn's place. You can get a look at Quinn, and we can recall old times together.'

O'Brien regarded him balefully. 'You can do the talking for both of us,' he remarked, 'while I put a couple steaks down.'

Smith shook his head through a grin. 'Jim Elder was right,' he commented. 'You're ornery as a grizzly after hibernation.'

O'Brien grunted as he left. 'That sweet talk won't get your supper paid for,' he said in his throat. Then he was gone.

CHAPTER EIGHT

McGraw and Lucas rode into town that evening, while O'Brien and Smith were having supper at Maynard Quinn's restaurant. They saw the sign outside Mrs Barstow's house that announced rooms for rent and rode up there, dismounted, and looked about them with distaste.

'What a stinkhole of a town!' Lucas grumbled. 'No hotel, a crummy-looking saloon, and that greasy spoon down the street. What would bring that hunter down here?'

'That ain't for us to worry over,' McGraw told him. 'We just got to make sure he's here. We'll get us a room for one night, and take a look around. Maybe he's bedded down right here.'

They entered the house and found the proprietor, and she gave them a room with two beds down the hall from Sarah. At that moment, Sarah was at the rear of the house in the dining room, having her evening meal. They inquired about O'Brien, and Mrs Barstow said a man fitting that description had brought Sarah there earlier.

'Well, it looks like this is trail's end,' McGraw said when they rode down to the hostelry to bed their horses. 'Now we just have to locate him.'

When they emerged from the hostelry later, Lucas

turned to McGraw. 'Did you see that big Appaloosa in there?'

McGraw nodded. 'So what?'

'That's O'Brien's horse.'

McGraw frowned at him. 'Are you certain?'

'I remember it from that night. I could pick it out of a herd. And that means he's still here.'

'Good. We'll start looking right away. If we have any trouble, that woman might know something. But you'll have to keep out of sight'

'Huh?'

'He knows you by sight, pea-brain. He'll know what's up soon as he sees you. You'll have to stick around the room while I check things out. You get the woman's name, and keep an eye on her; I'll be asking around for him.'

'That stage company is run by an old buffalo hunter. Maybe him and O'Brien know each other.'

McGraw nodded. 'Now you're thinking. I might check that out first. Just leave that to me. You stick to the room.'

'Sure. Anything you say, Corey.'

'That's right. Anything I say.'

Sarah hadn't seen O'Brien since he took her things into her room at Mrs Barstow's house. He had told her he would probably be staying in the area for a while, so she wondered where he would be sleeping, since he hadn't registered at Barstow's. She thought of the stage office then, because he knew the owner. So after her evening meal at Barstow's, which she found surprisingly palatable, she determined to walk down there while there was still some light in the sky.

O'Brien had just arrived there, just missing seeing McGraw and Lucas at the hostelry. Smith was making out some bills of lading when O'Brien arrived, but was ready to walk up Main Street past the saloon to Quinn's restaurant for supper with him. Smith had just seen a driver off on the Tulsa route, and had secured the corral and stables out back, so most of his work was finished for the evening. They set out for Quinn's place just after Sarah had left Barstow's, coming from the opposite direction. The sun was low in the sky, and had painted the horizon a dull yellow. Smith was giving O'Brien more details about the temporary marshal's job, and O'Brien listened with faint interest, as they made their way toward the restaurant.

By that time, Sarah had reached the area of the saloon, and One-Eye Wylie was just emerging from there as she approached, intent on riding out to Ben Driscoll's place to discuss future plans. Jake Latimer was expected to be there, too.

Wylie was about to descend some steps to a hitching rail when he saw Sarah approaching. He paused, squinted his good eye down, and turned to her as she walked up to pass him.

'Hey, hold on, little girlie. Where you headed at this late hour?' he asked, in a soft, sibilant voice.

She stopped just short of him, as he was blocking her path. 'I'm walking to the express office. Now, please let me pass.'

Wylie grinned a crooked grin and scared her. 'Why, there ain't no call to be in a hurry. Maybe you and me could talk a minute. You're new in town, ain't you? I ain't seen you before.'

Sarah was frustrated and frightened. Things like this didn't happen in Boston. 'Yes, I just arrived. I'm a friend of Mr Latimer. Now, please.'

Wylie's good eye widened slightly. 'Jake Latimer? Well, if that don't beat all! Jake and me do business together! You're that mail-order woman, ain't you?'

Sarah sighed, and tried to slip past him, but he moved, too.

'Say, how come you ain't in his bed tonight?' A gutteral laugh. 'Maybe you want to look the field over here first, heh? To see what else is available?'

'If you don't allow me to pass, I'll call for help,' she said firmly.

'Help? What do you want help for? We're just having a nice, quiet conversation, ain't we?'

But just at that moment O'Brien and Smith came up behind Wylie, and both assessed what was happening immediately. 'Hey, ain't that Miss Carter?' Smith said in a surprisingly soft voice.

O'Brien nodded just as Sarah spotted him. He came on up behind Wylie as Wylie continued his harrassment. 'Maybe you and me could walk a little together, missie. Latimer won't have to know.'

'You crude wretch!' Sarah blurted out. 'Get away from me!'

Wylie's face turned a dark color, and his good eye looked wild. 'Why, you back-east tramp! Maybe I'll just—'

O'Brien's Winchester was back at the stage office because Smith had asked him to leave it behind. But he now stepped forward nonchalantly, grabbed Wylie in both hands, and hurled him violently against the building wall.

Wylie hit it hard, making a loud crashing sound, and then slid to the boardwalk under their feet. He hadn't even noticed the two men behind him, and his face was full of shock now. He was breathing heavily, and his left arm felt as if it were broken, but it wasn't. His rib cage hurt, and rockets of pain raced through his head and into his back.

'What happened'?' he asked, gasping it out, dazed and confused.

89

'You just met O'Brien, Wylie,' Smith grinned.

'The lady told you to leave her alone,' O'Brien glared down at him. He kicked out savagely and connected with Wylie's right thigh, and Wylie cried out in further pain. But now he knew which man had attacked him.

'Stop, O'Brien,' Sarah said quietly.

Wylie now reached for the gun on his hip, still lying on his side, and aimed it at O'Brien's chest. 'You're a dead man!' he grated out.

'If you do that, Wylie, you're the dead man,' Smith warned him.

Wylie glanced at Smith through his pain and anger, and then back at O'Brien. When he saw the look of him, and the expression in O'Brien's eyes, he hesitated. Something about O'Brien made his mouth go dry. He lowered his Webley.

'I don't know who you are, mister. But nobody does this to me. Nobody.' He regained his feet awkwardly, and his right leg almost gave out under him.

'Leave the lady alone,' O'Brien growled at him. 'Or there'll be more of the same. Now, get out of here.'

Wylie hesitated another moment, cast a scathing look toward Sarah, and then limped away, holstering the gun. Smith had a big grin on his face. O'Brien walked over to Sarah. 'Are you OK?'

She looked into his square face, and smiled. 'I am now. You seem to have to keep rescuing me.'

O'Brien gave her a rare smile. 'You get into more trouble than any three women I ever met,' he told her. 'Where you headed?'

'I was just on my way to Mr Smith's office to see if you were there,' she said. 'I hadn't really thanked you properly for taking such good care of me. And now I'm even further obligated.'

90

'No, ma'am, you're not,' he said.

'That was One-Eye Wylie, ma'am,' Smith said in his loud voice. 'He's got as much morals as a cockroach.' He turned to O'Brien. 'You'll have to watch your back now. He'll be patient about it, but his aim will be to gun you down. He's a killer.'

'He won't be the first,' O'Brien said easily. 'Look, Sarah. We're heading down to Quinn's for some grub. Why don't you join us?'

'I've eaten, O'Brien,' she said. 'But I'll sit with you and have a cup of coffee.'

'That's just dandy, ma'am,' Smith grinned at her.

The three of them were given a table in a rear corner, and Maynard Quinn himself came out to take their order. He had used the robbery money to re-do the small restaurant, and was getting a few more customers.

'Shanghai,' he greeted Smith, standing over them with an apron on. 'I see you got some new friends here.'

Smith nodded. 'This here is Miss Sarah Carter,' he said. 'She come to town to marry Jake Latimer.' He watched Quinn's face.

Quinn showed surprise, then understanding. 'Oh, yeah. I heard of your coming, Miss Carter. I'm a good friend of Jake's.'

'Yeah, you and Wylie been hanging around with him and Ben Driscoll quite a bit,' Smith commented.

Quinn looked a little embarrassed. 'Oh, we have some card games. But Ben and Wylie keep pretty much to themselves.'

Sarah was absorbing all of this silently, watching O'Brien's face through it.

'This fellow over here is O'Brien,' Smith went on. 'Me and him used to hunt shaggies together.'

91

Quinn looked O'Brien over carefully, and when their eyes met for a moment, he felt immediately uncomfortable. 'Pleasured to meet both of you. Now, can I talk you into some of our rib-eye steak? It's the best in the Territory.'

The men ordered the steak, and Sarah requested coffee and a roll. When Quinn was gone, she turned to Smith. 'Did you say that that awful Wylie is a friend of Jake Latimer?'

O'Brien gave him a look. He had wanted Sarah to make her own judgment of Latimer, before impugning his character.

'Well, we don't know that, I guess,' Smith corrected himself. 'Let's say they're acquaintances.'

Sarah looked past him, reflecting on that information, and recalling how crude Latimer had seemed on their first meeting. 'I see,' she said slowly.

They were served shortly, and most of the meal was spent with Smith asking Sarah about herself, and Boston. She found that she liked this mountainous man who had hunted with O'Brien. And as for O'Brien, she was developing feelings for him which confused and alarmed her. She was beginning to find that she was strangely content and tranquil whenever he was with her. But it was more than that; her pulse quickened when he was near her, and when he spoke to her. She had never felt quite like that with a man.

When they were all through eating, Smith fell more silent with his big belly full. O'Brien was still thinking about the offer made to him by the mayor through Smith, and was even more quiet than usual. Sarah looked over at him.

'Your name sounds Irish, but you don't look Irish.'

O'Brien glanced over at her, coming out of deep thought. 'No, ma'am. My daddy took on our name when he come over here, because he had got into trouble back home. He was a Highlander Scot, and my mother was

Welsh. Both big people. My mother once almost killed a rogue Cherokee that wanted to steal her pies.' He chuckled in his throat, thinking of it.

'What's your first name?' she said. 'Do you mind telling me?'

'Oh, he don't tell no first name,' Smith quickly put in. 'Only a few know it.'

O'Brien looked over at her. He liked her face. There was strength in it. 'My mother named me Badrig,' he finally responded, embarrassed. 'It's Welsh, and I hate it.'

Sarah's face brightened. 'Why, it's a wonderful name!' she exclaimed.

'Don't never call me it,' he said seriously, looking down at the table.

In that moment, she felt a tenderness for him that was quite overwhelming. 'I won't, O'Brien. I never will.'

'Well, that sets a record,' Smith grinned, his ruddy, fat cheeks glowing. 'Dinner with a lady, and then this. He must like you, ma'am.'

O'Brien gave him a blistering look. 'Why don't you stick to making talk on stuff you know something about, fat man?'

Sarah saw his discomfiture, and was more embarrassed for him than for herself. 'We've eaten together before, Mr Smith,' she said. 'Out of necessity, out on the trail.'

'Sarah makes trail grub taste almost good,' O'Brien commented, taking a last drink of coffee.

Shanghai Smith furrowed his brow. That was the first time he had ever heard O'Brien compliment anybody.

Sarah didn't understand why, but for a moment her eyes started to tear up. Neither man noticed when she dabbed at one. 'I guess you must be staying with Mr Smith?' she said to O'Brien.

'He's got some cots out back,' O'Brien said. 'I'll have to take the mattress off and sleep on the springs or I'll pitch around all night.'

Smith laughed a fat-crowded laugh. 'I come into a hotel room one time and found him sleeping on the floor. The bed was still made up.'

Sarah found herself studying O'Brien's masculine face. Actually, under the beard and shaggy hair, he was a good-looking man, despite the beginning of gray in places. The thing that emanated from him was power. No, she thought, it was more than that. It was rock-steady certainty about himself, and who he was, and being completely comfortable with it.

'When will you start your trapping?' she asked him.

O'Brien glanced over at her. 'I reckon that's out now. It's no good here.'

'It's played out now,' Smith said. 'But we offered him work. We had a stage robbery the other day, with a killing. We think the bandits might be local.'

Sarah frowned. 'I'm sorry to hear that, Mr Smith. And it was one of your own coaches?'

'Yes, ma'am. I suspect that boy Wylie that was bothering you out on the street there might be involved in it. With a couple of others.' He looked over at O'Brien.

The connection didn't escape Sarah's attention. 'He said he was a friend of Jake Latimer,' she said quietly.

'Yes, ma'am,' Smith said.

'There's no evidence against Latimer, though, Sarah,' O'Brien put in.

'Yes, I understand,' she said soberly. She suddenly was acutely aware of the fact that Latimer was the only contact she had in town, after O'Brien was gone. Except for Shanghai Smith.

94

After a short silence, Smith said: 'Well, I had something to ask Mrs Barstow. Maybe you're ready to walk back there now, Miss Carter? We could all go.'

'Yes, I was about to leave,' Sarah said. 'O'Brien?'

'You got an escort, ma'am,' O'Brien said. 'I better go get my gear straightened away. You take good care of her, Smitty. I'll look you up before I leave here, Sarah.'

She was worried for him now. 'Be careful,' she said to him.

When they got out on the street, Sarah and Smith headed back toward the Barstow place, while O'Brien started down the other way. It was dark now, and he wished he had his Winchester with him. When he got to the stage office, he took his things out back to the dormitory-type room there where one of Smith's drivers was snoring loudly, making O'Brien wonder if he should just take his bedroll outside. But at least this got him out of the weather. He found a lower bunk, removed its soft mattress and leaned it against a wall, and left a thin pillow against the bare springs. A ticking wall clock in the office told him it was still quite early, so he decided to take a walk down to the stables to make sure the hostler had fed and tended the Appaloosa properly. As he left, he picked up the Winchester and cradled it under his right arm.

A cloudy sky was clearing, and a first-quarter moon was edging out from behind a high bank of cloud cover. Glancing up at it, it seemed like an old friend to him. Wherever he was on the trail, from Montana to Texas, it had always kept him company on nights when the only sounds on the prairie were the wail of a coyote or the singing of the wind in the cottonwoods.

As O'Brien headed down to the hostelry, Corey McGraw and Wade Lucas were just emerging from the building.

McGraw had forgotten to tell the hostler that he wanted a shoe replaced on his horse. Now he was heading back to deposit Lucas at Mrs Barstow's house while he looked around town for O'Brien. But he and Lucas hadn't taken ten steps from the stables when Lucas squinted down and stared up the dirt street toward town.

'I don't believe it!' he gasped out.

McGraw frowned. 'What?'

'It's him! Coming down the street right at us! See, it's a good thing I was with you. You'd never have spotted him.'

'That's O'Brien? Well, well. Maybe this can be over faster than I thought.'

'What will we do?' Lucas asked anxiously.

McGraw looked behind him. 'The hostler just rode off home. This is a perfect chance for us. Come on, before he sees you. We'll hide around that corner of the building. He'll be very close to us. We'll wait till he heads into the stables, and we have his back. Then we'll both open fire. By the time anybody knows what happened, we'll be saddled up and gone from here.'

Lucas licked suddenly dry lips, and nodded uncertainly. 'I'll follow your lead.'

'Let me fire first. I want to tell Emmet I killed him.'

Lucas nodded again, and they retreated to the far corner of the building, past the big open doorway. Now O'Brien was only a block away, his thoughts on Sarah Carter, realizing the danger she might be in if Latimer was an outlaw. He hadn't seen the two men, and was still preoccupied with Sarah when he reached the building and stopped just outside the doorway.

'Hallo there! Anybody here?'

He could dimly see his Appaloosa in a stall inside, so stepped on in to take a look at it. At that moment, McGraw

96

came out of hiding, Lucas just behind him; they walked to the doorway and saw O'Brien's back.

O'Brien thought he heard the sound of footfalls on gravel, but figured it must be the hostler. As he started to turn, though, a gunshot rang out behind him and he felt a blow to his back that almost felled him. He had been hit by McGraw's shot in the high ribs, and it dizzied him for a moment as pain shot through his torso. But despite that trauma, he turned and fired the Winchester at the first target he saw, which was McGraw.

The rifle exploded loudly in the barn, and then fired a second time. McGraw was hit in the middle and lower chest, and went dancing backwards into Lucas, knocking Lucas down. McGraw was dead when he hit the ground, and Lucas's Adams .42 went off as they hit, firing into the ceiling of the building. O'Brien staggered against a stall post, trying to focus on Lucas, but Lucas had scrambled to his feet and was running off into the night.

O'Brien leaned against the post then, feeling the wetness on his back and the shock beginning to numb him, and knew he had to get help. After a long moment, he pushed himself off the post and staggered back outside. The moon was still looking down on him but he didn't see it. He felt very faint for a moment, but then forced himself to walk. It was a long way to the town center. But he kept walking. Staggering and stumbling.

Halfway to the first lighted building, where he thought he might find help, he collapsed into the dirt street on his face.

CHAPTER NINE

When Shanghai Smith returned from Mrs Barstow's place, O'Brien had been lying lifeless in the street for fifteen minutes. A couple of cowhands had come out of the saloon up the street, but neither had seen the prone figure in the darkness. Now Smith stopped thirty yards from O'Brien and squinted down, and immediately recognized the rawhides, and the look of the inert form.

'O'Brien?' With shortness of breath, he thundered on down the street, making the ground shake with his weight. 'O'Brien!'

A moment later he was kneeling beside his friend, turning him over. O'Brien's face was ashen, and he didn't appear to be breathing. But Smith felt for a pulse, and found one in his throat. His hand was wet from where he had grabbed O'Brien's back. 'It's that snake-in-the-grass Wylie!' he grated out. He gently slapped O'Brien's face, and there was a low groan in his chest.

'Yeah, that's my boy!' Smith gushed, his ruddy cheeks even more red. 'You stick with me, old friend. We're going to get you through this!'

O'Brien came around, his eyelids slowly opening. 'It wasn't Wylie,' he said thickly. 'Some men was after me. One of them is laying dead at the stables. The other one cut and run.'

'Don't talk,' Smith said urgently. 'I'll get help.'

'My Winchester is back there, too.'

'Stay quiet,' Smith insisted. He saw a man emerge from a house up the street, and called out to him. 'Over here! A shot man!'

There was no doctor in Fort Revenge, but there was a veterinarian who had treated gunshot wounds in the past. In a few minutes there were three other men beside O'Brien, and they got him on to a blanket and carried him up the street to the vet's house. Soon O'Brien was inside on a bed, with the vet digging the Smith & Wesson slug from his back. By late evening it was done, and O'Brien was resting easy on the vet's recovery bed. The bullet had punctured a lung, but that was already healing, because of the buffalo man's remarkable recovery powers.

Within ten minutes of the shoot-out, Wade Lucas had stolen a horse and ridden out of town, very scared and wondering if O'Brien had recognized him. By morning, when O'Brien was awake and already asking for coffee, Lucas had arrived in a small town west of Fort Revenge, where he stopped at a telegraph station and wired Emmet Purcell that McGraw was dead, and that O'Brien might still be alive. In the same telegram, Lucas tendered his resignation from Purcell's employ, and said he was headed for Texas to find work as a drover. Actually, he planned to ride to California, where he hoped O'Brien would never see him again.

By mid-morning on that day, O'Brien was sitting up in bed and talking to Smith about his future.

'Well, I already talked to Mayor Spencer,' Smith was telling O'Brien. 'I told him you wouldn't be pinning no badge on now. You should be dead, and any other man would be. I still don't know how you walked up the street with that bullet in you.'

O'Brien was sitting against a pillow, bare-chested, with a large bandage circling his torso. He looked very muscular sitting there, very hard. 'Don't you remember what the Lakota used to say?' he grinned. 'Bullets bounce off me, Smitty.'

Smith made a sour face, looking at the other scars on O'Brien's body. 'Looks like a couple of them made their way through that tough hide.'

'Did that horse doctor really get that lead out of me?'

'He did a good job. You couldn't have lasted long with that in you like that. I give him a good fee; he probably won't work for a month now. He says you ought to keep to bed for a couple weeks. He'll put you up right here.'

O'Brien shook his shaggy head. 'I'll be up in a day or two. I been stung by wasps worse than this. I got plans to make.'

'You can't go trapping in your condition.'

'I been thinking. I need a grubstake, and now I owe you. Maybe I'll stick around for a while, if Spencer's offer is still open.'

'Are you crazy? If you can't go trapping, you sure can't do any lawing. You won't be fit to stand up to stone killers, buffalo man. They'll put you six feet under next time.'

'I don't want no badge. I don't want to work under the color of the law. But I'll give Spencer two weeks, at the rate of pay he mentioned. That will give me enough to travel south and find new grounds.'

Smith grunted. 'I doubt if Spencer would put any money on you now. We won't be able to convince him you'll be worth the investment.'

'Then I'll get my gear together and ride out. I'll get by.'

Smith took a deep breath in. 'I got a better idea. You can work for me for two weeks when you're on your feet. Spencer would expect me to share the expense, anyway, since it's my business in danger. You can work off the vet's fee and have enough over to pay your way south.'

'Can you afford that?'

Smith was sitting on a hard chair beside the bed. He laced his pudgy fingers together now, and sighed. 'I think we're dealing with Ben Driscoll here. And since he took that first stage so easy, I think he'll keep hitting them now till he puts me right out of business. I can't afford not to hire you, partner. Didn't we always work good together on the trail? You grubstaked me a couple of times. Now we'll work together again to stop these robberies. Of course, we'll have to catch them in the act.'

'Maybe ride the coaches ourselves?' O'Brien suggested, grimacing in pain as he adjusted himself on the pillow.

'That's right. Now, I figure they'll only hit the ones carrying payroll. There's another shipment coming up soon, and it would be a big haul; a payroll coming from a bank in Tulsa through here and on to the bank in Scobeyville. We could sneak on the coach in the dark when it leaves here in mid-evening, so Driscoll wouldn't know. Then the next morning at Tulsa, when we leave there with the payroll, we would pull other ticketed passengers off and make them take the next stage through. You could ride shotgun, you're the Webster with guns. Me and a second driver would be in the coach, to surprise Driscoll's gang. It would be four against four. What do you think?'

O'Brien looked over at him gravely. 'I think you was one of the best shaggy hunters that ever rode along the Upper Platte. But you might get yourself killed in a close-up gunfight, partner. You don't move fast enough. You can't go.'

Smith's beefy face crimsoned. 'Now wait just a mustang minute here! This here company belongs to me, remember, and that gives me the right to defend it!'

There was a tense silence in the room, hanging like lead weights over their heads. Then O'Brien spoke again.

'I ain't arguing this, Smitty. This is my show. I won't help you get your stubborn head blowed off. And I wouldn't want no second driver in the coach, neither. Most of your people probably can't hit the door of a coach standing beside it. Pick out your best man with a gun and I'll ride shotgun for him. And like you said, we'll pull off passengers at Tulsa.'

Smith was angry. 'Did you forget you're working for me?'

'If you go, I won't,' O'Brien said evenly.

Smith scowled at him.

'You're paying me to put an end to this, and this is the way I want it. If things go wrong, you won't owe me nothing.'

Smith got up from beside O'Brien's bed and stalked around the room for several minutes, grumbling in his throat while O'Brien watched him. Finally he turned back to O'Brien. 'If they get that shipment, I'm done.'

'I figured that.'

'Well, I must be crazy. But if you get on your feet in time, we'll do it your way.'

O'Brien managed a half-grin. 'Good decision, partner.' He started to continue, when the bedroom door opened and the vet looked in. He was a small, emaciated-looking fellow wearing spectacles.

'Mr O'Brien. There's a lady here to see you. Shall I show her in?'

Smith rose from his chair. 'It's got to be Sarah. I'll just make room for her in here. Bring her in, Doc.'

O'Brien gave him a sour look. He didn't want any visitors. 'Yeah, send her in.' He quickly pulled on a dungaree shirt lent to him by the vet, and fastened a couple of buttons through stabbing pain.

Sarah came in a moment later, meeting Smith at the door as he left. He tipped his hat, greeting her with a grin, and whispered that O'Brien was all right. Then he was gone and Sarah and O'Brien were alone.

She came over to the bed and looked down at him, and he saw her eyes tear up. She saw the thick bandage showing between the buttons.

'Oh, heavens,' she choked out.

'I'm all right, Sarah.'

'I came as soon as I heard, at breakfast earlier.'

'The vet is taking good care of me.'

She wiped at a tear. 'I thought you were invulnerable. The way you always handled yourself.'

He smiled. 'I'm not sure what that means. But I'll be up from here in no time. Smitty give me a job.'

'A job?' she wondered. 'In your condition?'

'Just riding on one of his stages, ma'am. It's not like busting broncos.'

'Who did this? The men from the ranch you mentioned?'

'That's what it looks like. But it's over now.'

'Will they send others?' Her pretty face was tense.

'I doubt it. I ain't that important to them. Have you seen Latimer again?'

'He came past Mrs Barstow's this morning, just before I started over here. He talked to Mayor Spencer, and said he can marry us later today.'

'Oh,' O'Brien said. 'I didn't think it would be that soon.'

'I told him I'd just heard you were shot, and didn't want to think about it right now.' She looked down. 'He became quite agitated. Not polite at all. He said I could have another day or two. Then he'd drag me down to the mayor's office if he had to. He talked a lot about our promises to each other, and how he needed me at the farm. He said it wasn't up to me now. His tone was a little menacing. More so than at the farm that day. I don't think I can hold him off much longer.'

'Do you want to?' he asked.

She shook her head uncertainly. 'He's not at all what I expected. And now I find he's in with some shady characters. But on the other hand, he's all I have here. If I don't marry Jake, I'm on my way back to Boston. If he'll allow me to leave.'

O'Brien stared past her. 'I didn't like that boy at first sight. But you have to make your own decisions, Sarah. I wouldn't want to get between you and your dreams.'

'But I want your advice,' she told him. 'I respect your judgment more than any other person's.'

He hesitated. 'Well. I expect Latimer might be the type to hurt a wife, even if he ain't violating no laws with Driscoll. He just seemed a mite mean to me. I reckon you can do a whole lot better. Any man would be lucky to stand up with you and tie the knot.'

'Really, O'Brien?' she asked him, looking into his blue eyes.

'Well. Any man that takes to married life,' he qualified it, not understanding her interest.

'I guess you're not that kind of man.'

He looked startled. 'Oh, no, ma'am. I live on the trail. I don't own no land, never have much of a bank account, and don't expect nothing from the world. A woman has to have a home, ma'am. I can't give it to her.'

'You won't be hunting and trapping forever. Will you?'

104

O'Brien shrugged his wide shoulders, and felt pain again. 'I don't know much else, Sarah. I'll probably die alone out on some hot flat of sand, with turkey vultures tearing at my carcass.'

'It doesn't have to be that way,' she insisted.

'Well. Good thing we can't see very far ahead, I reckon. We might not like the view.'

There it was again, she thought. The flash of frontier sagacity showing through the illiterate speech. He was much more knowledgeable and had greater insight into the way things were than his appearance or his manner announced. She found herself wishing his answer to her had been different, that he had given her some hope for a deeper relationship with him than she had at present. She began to wish it was O'Brien she was committed to, rather than that good-looking but intimidating Jake Latimer.

She touched his arm affectionately. 'I'll bring you some soup this afternoon,' she promised him. 'You should try to get some rest now.'

O'Brien regarded her curiously. He had never had a woman worry over him or show him tenderness since his Welsh mother. 'You don't have to bother with that,' he said. 'I'll probably be eating beef tomorrow.'

'Nevertheless,' she smiled. 'You can expect me back later today.'

'Yes, ma'am,' he said quietly.

A moment later she was gone, with him staring soberly after her.

At that same time up north at the Purcell ranch, Emmet Purcell was in his library studying the telegram he had received from Wade Lucas. Beside him was an acting foreman who had replaced McGraw in his absence. His

105

name was Duke Hawley and he was Purcell's best bronco buster. He was also an expert with guns, and had run afoul of the law before joining Purcell. For his part, Purcell had little respect for the law, anyway. He made his own law in his area, and liked having men around him who could handle themselves with guns. In Purcell's view, might made right, and in his mind he was always right.

He looked up gravely from the telegram. 'I wanted you to hear this. That hunter killed McGraw. Down in Fort Revenge.'

Hawley creased his dark brow. He was tall and lanky, and was known to be a rather moody, aloof fellow. 'McGraw is dead?'

'I should have sent you after that sub-human animal,' Purcell said heavily. 'As it is, McGraw failed to get the job done and that killer of Tully is still alive. Every breath he takes mocks us, Duke. Mocks me. And that coward Lucas ran off to Texas. If I ever see him again, I'll personally put a bullet in his yellow hide.'

'Are we sure the hunter is still alive?'

'Lucas thought so, and he told me that despite his yellow streak. I'd say we still got a job to do. To avenge Tully's death.'

Hawley nodded. He had narrow, hard eyes and a broken nose. 'Send me down there. I'll clean it up for you real quick.' He laid his hand on the protruding Starr .44 on his hip.

Purcell shook his head. 'I'm not taking any chances this time. I'm going down there with you. And I won't leave there till that low-life is pushing up daisies at the local cemetery.'

'I'm ready to ride when you are,' Hawley said.

'It will take me a few days to wind up some things here.

Then we'll ride south. When we find him, I want to put the first bullet in him. I know how to do it so he'll die slow. For Tully.'

Hawley tipped his black Stetson lower over his dark eyes. 'Just give me the word when you're ready to ride.'

Over the next several days O'Brien healed from the back wound. The vet who treated him couldn't believe that he was up and walking around on the second day after being shot. Sarah brought him soup and hot food several times over that week, and then O'Brien moved back in with Smith and his drivers at the stage depot. O'Brien now was aware of Sarah's increasing interest in him, but didn't know how to handle it. Women just had no place in his life, but he wasn't sure she understood that yet.

Several things happened in that week while O'Brien healed: Shanghai Smith delayed taking the payroll shipment until O'Brien felt strong again; Mayor Avery Spencer volunteered to contribute some of the town council's treasury to help defray Smith's cost of making a stand against robbery; and lastly, Latimer grew impatient with Sarah, came to get her at the Barstow place, and ended up shouting insults at her when she refused to leave with him.

'You ain't got no say-so in this, missy! You're bought and paid for, and you're mine now, whether you changed your mind or not! You don't come down here and tease a man like you might in Boston! Now, you're coming to my bed tonight, marriage certificate or not!'

He wouldn't leave without Sarah until Mrs Barstow took a small revolver from her apron and threatened him with it. But he promised to be back, and left hurling insults at Sarah and Barstow. When he was gone, Sarah made up her mind for good: she could not marry such a man, even if that left her alone and friendless here in the West.

O'Brien ached whenever he moved, but less and less with each day that passed. To Smith's wonderment, by the fifth day he was doing exercises to improve his strength and promote healing. O'Brien was wearing just a small bandage on his back now, and had stopped bleeding through it. He knew that the wound would give him minor trouble for months, but he figured he would be ready to ride shotgun when the payroll run was scheduled, which was just a few days off now. He didn't look beyond that; you couldn't make long plans in his world.

Out at Ben Driscoll's shack near town, he and his three partners in crime had just heard about the payroll run from one of Smith's drivers, who had let the news slip purposely, and Driscoll's appetite was whetted again. He now paced the small cabin floor animatedly, discussing the situation with the others. Wylie was leaning against a nearby wall, and Quinn and Latimer were seated at a small table on straight chairs.

'We don't have a lot of information yet,' Driscoll was saying. 'But this haul could be even bigger. This one will stop here from Tulsa, but take the gold on over to Scobeyville. That's usually a big payroll for the ranches around here.'

'I like it,' Jake Latimer said. He was still smarting from his encounter with Sarah, and embarrassed because they all knew about his trouble with her. 'I'm in.'

Driscoll cast a sour look his way. 'The ruins of the old fort are just a few miles outside of town. They would make perfect cover for us. We can hit the stage there, and be back here for dinner.'

Quinn looked up at him. 'That's pretty close to town, Ben. Somebody might see us coming back from it.'

'Ain't it nice to have a real expert here?' Wylie said with sarcasm. He still had a sore rib from his encounter with O'Brien.

Quinn shot a cold look at him as Driscoll continued. 'It's obvious we'll have to take a long route back, Maynard,' he said. 'Wylie and me will come back here, and you and Latimer can go on home. We'll divide it up later.'

'That sounds good,' Quinn agreed.

'Then it's all set,' Driscoll told them. 'We'll meet right here that morning, for final arrangements. This might be a big one.'

'Big is what I want,' Latimer put in with a small grin.

Wylie looked over at him. 'At least you won't have to worry over that woman stealing it from you,' he grinned. 'I hear she turned you down cold.'

Latimer's square face went straight-lined. 'I don't care if I marry her now. I'm just going to go over there and take her home with me. And when I get her there, she'll learn the facts of life.'

'You need any help taming her, I'm always available,' Wylie grinned. 'I took a liking to her the other night, and I think she felt the same. Maybe she'd like to come home with me.'

'You keep away from her, scar-face,' Latimer growled at him. 'That's my property!'

'Or maybe she's the property of that buffalo hunter,' Quinn grinned. 'Oh, I guess you all know he got back-shot down at the hostler's. Somebody from out of town. He might not ever recover, so I guess your competition is gone now, Latimer.'

'That hunter is the one attacked me in the street,' Wylie said sullenly. 'If he don't die, I might just finish the job myself.'

109

'You won't do nothing of the kind,' Driscoll said harshly. 'Not as long as you're working with me. He don't mean nothing to us.'

'Well, what about this?' Wylie retorted. 'I hear he's been hired by Smith.'

Driscoll frowned. 'Are you sure?'

'One of the mayor's stable hands told me.'

Driscoll stood there thinking. 'He must not be so bad off after all. I reckon he'd be good with a gun. Maybe Smith wants him to ride shotgun.'

'I hope so,' Wylie said quietly. 'I hope he's on our run.'

Latimer looked over at him. 'Yeah, in his wounded condition, Wylie, it would be like shooting a turkey in a barrel, wouldn't it?'

'OK, boys,' Driscoll intervened. 'Two men on the box won't make no difference. They'll both be dead as soon as they throw their guns down. Now, I'll see you all back here that morning. Don't make me wait.'

'We'll be here, Ben,' Maynard Quinn assured him.

CHAPTER TEN

It was only a couple of days now until the Tulsa run. O'Brien had taken the Appaloosa out into the countryside for a couple of rides, to get limbered up, and was doing exercises out in back of Smith's depot, beside the corral. Smith watched in fascination as O'Brien grew in strength and stamina. Nobody he had ever known could have come back from that trauma so quickly. After a week of recovery, O'Brien had been strapping harness on teams for Smith, and repairing broken parts of coaches, just to keep moving around. Then he was down at the hostler's, oiling his saddle and cleaning the Appaloosa's shoes.

On the day before the big Tulsa run, the mayor stopped in at the stage depot and found O'Brien and Smith having a cup of coffee in Smith's office, which adjoined the waiting room for passengers. There were several passengers waiting for one of Smith's coaches to come in. Spencer walked past them and through the open doorway to Smith's office. O'Brien and Smith were seated at Smith's littered desk, talking.

'Gentlemen,' Spencer greeted them.

'Mr Mayor,' Smith boomed out. 'Come on in and have a cup of java!'

'I just had breakfast,' Spencer said. He leaned against the wall just inside the doorway. 'How's that back wound healing, O'Brien?'

O'Brien glanced up at him. 'I don't even feel it now, Mayor.' He still wore a very small bandage over the wound, but it had stopped draining and was healing over.

Spencer nodded, removed his hat, and ran a hand through his thinning hair. 'I got to admit I was wrong about you. I thought you'd still be on your back. Do you really think you're up to that run tomorrow?'

'One day we was out on a hunt,' Smith answered for him. 'O'Brien was knocked off his mount and run over in a stampede. Broke some ribs and cut him up some. But he was back on that herd after two nights of rest.'

O'Brien regarded him gravely. 'Never mind, Smitty.'

'I picked out Joe Reece to drive the run,' Smith went on. 'He's got some experience with a gun. R.C. Funk volunteered, but he'd shoot hisself in the foot.'

Spencer looked over at O'Brien. 'You know, it's not just Smith here who's counting on this going well,' he said slowly. 'If these people knock Smith out of business, this town might just wither up and die.'

O'Brien cast a stony look at him and took a swig of coffee. 'Maybe you'd rather go yourself, Mayor.'

Spencer's face changed. 'I didn't mean anything by that. But maybe you do need a couple more armed men in the coach with you. The last time, there were four riders attacking the stage. That don't seem like good odds.'

'That would just be two more boys to get shot up,' O'Brien told him. 'Any other suggestions?' he said, looking down at his tin coffee cup.

Spencer sighed, and shoved himself off the wall. He adjusted his glasses on his nose. 'I just hope you boys know what you're doing.'

He left then without further comment, and Smith looked over at O'Brien. 'He's nervous as a raccoon caught in a bear cage. But he did say some things I still got flying around in my head.'

O'Brien rose from his chair and replaced his Stetson. 'I'm going to walk over to Barstow's place. I didn't thank Sarah proper-like for bringing me all that grub.'

That was another first for O'Brien, Smith thought. 'Sure, partner. You want to thank her.' A chubby grin.

O'Brien turned and frowned at him. 'You know, Smitty. You always did act just like a jackass at times.'

Smith burst out in uproarious laughter, and slapped his thick thigh.

'Hee-haw! Hee-haw!' he roared out, and the laughter continued.

Sarah Carter had just returned to her room from the midday meal at Mrs Barstow's dining room. She knew her future was very much in doubt now, and had been thinking about it quite a lot. But she had also been tending O'Brien in his healing, and helping Shanghai Smith straighten out his account books, since she had done that kind of thing occasionally at the library in Boston.

Now, on this sunny April afternoon, she had decided to take her mind off things by taking out one of the books she had brought with her and reading some Jane Austen. She was just beginning the third chapter of *Mansfield Park* when a loud knocking came at her door. When she went to open it, Jake Latimer stood there.

'Oh!' she said, slightly startled. 'It's you.'

'It's me,' he said gruffly, pushing past her into the room. She was a little frightened, remembering how he had acted the last time there. She left the door open, and turned to him.

'What is it, Mr Latimer?' she asked coolly.

He faced her, his handsome face grim. 'Your little game is over now, Sarah. You're getting hitched today.'

She took a deep breath in. She was wearing a green, snug-fitting dress that showed her figure off to advantage, and her dark hair was caught up over her rather pretty face. She looked good to him.

'I should have told you this the last time you were here,' she said in a firm voice. 'I've given it some thought, Mr Latimer, and I can't marry you.'

A dark frown crawled on to his square face. 'Can't marry me? What can you be thinking, girl? I paid to get you here. I own you, missy, just like I own them chickens in my coop out back. I'm here to take you down to the mayor today, or else home with me. You got your choice.'

'Do you think I would live in sin with you?' she said defiantly. 'I told you, Mr Latimer. You and I are not suited. I don't like your crass manner, and the way you try to intimidate me. I'm a free and independent citizen, Mr Latimer, and have the right to make my own decisions about my life. I promise to re-pay you for any financial loss you suffered in this transaction.'

He came very close to her, and shouted into her face. 'We have a contract! And I mean to see that you honor it!'

'You withheld information from me. Our contract is null and void! But I will reimburse you, as soon as I'm on my feet again.'

Suddenly he drew the big Colt .44 on his hip, and placed its muzzle up against her breastbone. With the other hand he grabbed her right arm so hard that it made her gasp in pain. 'Now. That's all the talk there'll be about it. I'm taking

114

you home. I don't need no marriage certificate. You're bought property, lady. Let's go.'

Sarah was now terrified. 'No! Shoot me now if you're taking me home!' She writhed in the pain from his iron grip. 'I'd rather be dead!'

Latimer grinned a diamond-hard grin. 'That ain't your choice either,' he said in a low, even voice.

But in that moment, O'Brien appeared in the open doorway. Latimer heard his spurs, and turned quickly, releasing his hold on Sarah. O'Brien filled the doorway like a rampant grizzly. Under his right arm was the Winchester he almost always carried with him.

'What's going on here?' he asked casually.

'Oh. The hunter,' Latimer said to himself. 'Look, O'Brien. This ain't your business any more. This is between me and the girl.' He still held the Colt in his gun hand, but had dropped it to his side.

O'Brien looked past him to Sarah, 'Are you OK?' he said to her.

'He wants me to go home with him. But I don't want to,' she said. 'I've decided I can't marry him.'

O'Brien moved into the room, watching Latimer carefully, wondering if he would be confronting him out on the stage trail tomorrow. 'That sounds pretty cut and dried,' he said. 'The lady don't want nothing to do with you. You had your chance with her, mister. Now you ought to let it go.'

Latimer turned and grabbed Sarah's arm again, and made her cry out softly. 'Now I'm taking this woman home with me, hunter. I don't know what you two had going between you out there on the trail, and I ain't asking. But now that's over, and she's coming where she belongs. With me.'

O'Brien barred his path, standing between him and the

115

doorway. 'Boy, you got more brass than brains. But maybe I didn't make myself clear. You're either leaving here alone, or not at all.'

Latimer was very frustrated and angry. He raised the muzzle of the Colt, aiming it at O'Brien's midsection. 'Get out of my way.'

O'Brien stood there, and now the Winchester was aimed at Latimer's legs. 'Let go of her,' he said in a low growl.

Latimer hesitated. All he had to do was squeeze the trigger twice to fill the hunter with hot lead. But the look that had come over O'Brien's face, and the mere proximity of him, big and primordial, made the Colt slippery in his grasp.

After a moment, he lowered the Colt, and slid it back into its holster. Sarah pulled loose from him, and he let her go. She rubbed at her arm, frowning.

'You think you got something real nice going on here, huh?' Latimer now said to O'Brien. 'This ain't over, you know. This woman is mine.'

'Stay away from her, or you'll answer to me,' O'Brien told him.

'We'll see how it works out,' Latimer said in a tight voice. Then he brushed past O'Brien, brusquely storming from the room.

Sarah slumped into herself. She was trembling inside. O'Brien set his rifle against the wall and went over to her. 'You don't look so good.'

To his great surprise, she fell against him, sobbing, her arms around his neck. 'I've been such a fool!' she cried against his shoulder. 'I was desperate to make a life somehow. I should have stayed in Boston. At least I had friends there.'

O'Brien didn't know what to do. He didn't have to

116

comfort women in his small universe. He put a hand on her arm. 'I admire what you did – leaving Boston, looking for something better. Reminds me of me, when I was sixteen, setting out from the Shenandoah, to find out what I was.'

She looked up at him, her eyes and cheeks wet. 'I feel very . . . close to you, O'Brien.'

'I reckon that's natural, Sarah. We been through a lot together. You'd feel that way about anybody you rode with.'

'No. It's more than that,' she said. 'I have this all-aquiver feeling now whenever I'm around you. You have this emotional effect on me. Do you feel anything like that?'

O'Brien had to admit he had felt stirrings inside him when she smiled at him, or brought him soup, or touched him. He was also seeing her face before him when he was falling asleep at night.

He removed his hand from her arm. 'I don't think much about my feelings, ma'am,' he said awkwardly.

She pushed away from him, wiping at an eye. 'I shouldn't have asked you that. I don't know what's the matter with me. I'm very sorry, O'Brien. I've traded on our friendship. It won't happen again.'

'Don't think like that,' he told her, looking at the floor. 'I don't know how to talk to women, Sarah. I don't even know how to feel about women. This is all new and strange to me. I ain't had a good talk with a woman since my mother died. It ain't your fault. About my feelings, all I can think of to say is, I like you. I like you better than most men I meet.' He stood there mulling over what he had just said, and trying to make sense of it. 'Now, I came here to thank you. For all the kind attention at the vet's place. I ain't used to it, and I'm plumb awkward at things like this. But I figure you'll take the measure of it.'

'You're not awkward,' Sarah said, looking into his eyes.

'You're quite wonderful, to me. I'd be hard put to find a flaw in you,' she said, her voice breaking.

He was frowning heavily. 'Sarah.'

'There I go again. Just excuse me. Anyway, you don't need to thank me. It's me who owes gratitude; the way you stood up to Latimer, and all the rest. I'll always be grateful.'

O'Brien was becoming very uncomfortable. He tipped his Stetson and retrieved his rifle. 'We'll talk again, Sarah.'

'I hope so,' she said. 'Incidentally, I heard you're going to ride on one of Smith's stage routes soon.'

'The Tulsa run, tomorrow,' he said.

'Really? Are you well enough? And isn't it risky? Smith just had a stage held up and a driver killed.'

O'Brien tried a small grin. 'I'm just fine. And we know the risk. Sarah, I don't need nobody fretting over me. I ain't used to it.'

She sighed. 'I can't seem to say anything right today. But please be careful. I'll be watching for your return.'

'I'll see you then,' he told her.

When he turned and disappeared down the corridor, his riding spurs clanking in the narrow confines of the place, she wondered if she would ever see him again.

That was what it was like, knowing O'Brien. You always took a good look at that ruggedly handsome face when he left you, you never knew for sure if it was for the last time.

CHAPTER ELEVEN

That evening O'Brien and Smith went down the street again to Quinn's restaurant and ordered T-bone steaks and potatoes. O'Brien was feeling good now. The healing scar pulled at him sometimes, but otherwise he felt little residue from the gunshot wound.

Smith had a two-fold purpose in eating at Quinn's at the last moment before the Tulsa run: Quinn fried the best steaks for miles around, but also Smith wanted to watch Quinn's face to find any clues as to his participation in a possible hold-up on the upcoming run.

When O'Brien and Smith were seated at a side wall, there were three other customers already eating their supper there, all local ranchers and ranch-hands. They paid no attention to O'Brien or Smith. Quinn came out and took their orders himself, and seemed particularly friendly.

'Well, look here! Two of my favorite customers! What can I do for you tonight, boys? I got a terrific beef stew back there that you can wallop down with a plate of fresh corn dodgers!'

He wore a big, white apron over his work clothes, and looked like anything but an outlaw. But Smith suspected his close relationship with Ben Driscoll made him a prime suspect.

'We're going to live it up big tonight, Maynard,' Smith told him loudly. 'You can fry us up two of them T-bones you're always bragging about. And make them rare and raw!'

'Glad to see you up and about,' Quinn said to O'Brien. They hadn't been in since his being shot. 'You're looking real good.'

O'Brien looked up into his squinty green eyes. Quinn's red hair stuck out from under a white chef's hat and gave him a comical look. He met the open stare of O'Brien and swallowed slightly. O'Brien just nodded.

A moment later Quinn was gone, and Smith turned to O'Brien. 'Did you see that? He looked guilty as sin!'

Before O'Brien could reply, the front door opened and Ben Driscoll came in. When he saw Smith and O'Brien, he came right over to their table. 'Well, look who's here! I didn't know you could afford Maynard's high prices, Smith! Who's your friend here?'

Smith nodded soberly. 'This is O'Brien, Driscoll. He brought the Carter woman here with him when he come. We used to hunt together.'

Driscoll looked down at O'Brien, assessing the look of him. 'Pleasure to meet you, O'Brien. I hear you're driving for Smith now.'

O'Brien looked him over with distaste. 'You hear a lot.'

'O'Brien might spell some drivers,' Smith explained quickly. 'He needs to pick up some quick cash for his trapping.'

'Oh, you're a trapper,' Driscoll said. That seemed to verify what Quinn and Wylie had told him about O'Brien. He now remembered how Wylie had heard that O'Brien had made the famous Bill Longley back down once. He looked over at the Winchester rifle leaning against a chair

120

near O'Brien. 'I guess you must be pretty good with that long gun. But you don't carry a sidearm.'

O'Brien looked up at him with a fixed gaze. 'Why don't you take a load off? We got room here.'

Driscoll was surprised. 'Why, don't mind if I do. Smith?'

Smith shot a look at O'Brien. 'Sure. It will take our steaks a few minutes to fry. Set it down, Driscoll.'

Driscoll sat down near O'Brien, and continued to look him over. O'Brien ignored it, and swigged some coffee. 'I almost never had no need for a short gun,' he finally told Driscoll. 'The shaggies won't usually let you get that close. I see you favor a Remington.'

Driscoll slid the revolver out of its oiled holster with a fluid movement, and turned it over in his hand. 'I like the balance.' He twirled it around his trigger finger three times and let it nestle back into his grasp, but with the butt toward O'Brien. 'Care to get the feel?'

O'Brien put his hands up defensively. 'I reckon that's too much gun for me, Driscoll. I ain't no gunman.'

Driscoll smiled at those remarks. He slid the Remington .44 back into its resting place. 'I guess a gun's as big as the man handling it.'

'I hear tell that you're pretty good with it,' O'Brien offered.

'Oh, I know where to oil it,' Driscoll grinned.

'I got myself a Schofield, but it just sets on my mount's irons most of the time,' O'Brien told him.

'I'd like to see it sometime. I always wanted a Schofield.' A short pause. 'So you'll just be filling in for other drivers then, O'Brien?' he said casually.

O'Brien studied Driscoll's premature silver hair, and his brawny look. At a bit over forty, he was about O'Brien's age. O'Brien had registered in his head the fact that Driscoll carried a Remington revolver. It was light and fast, but not as accurate as a Colt, or O'Brien's Schofield. 'That's right,' O'Brien answered him. 'It's just temporary. I need a grub-stake to head south.'

'I probably won't be able to give him a run for a while,' Smith put in, hoping Driscoll believed him. 'But there's plenty of work to do around the depot.'

Driscoll nodded. 'I reckon there would be.' He turned to see Quinn bringing their meals, and Quinn stared hard when he saw him sitting with them. 'Well, here come your meals, boys.'

Quinn put the plates down, looking nervous. 'I hope they're done to your liking, gentlemen.' He glanced over at Driscoll furtively.

But Smith broke the tension. 'I reckon you two don't need no introduction,' he boomed out. 'I hear you play a lot of cards together.'

'That's right,' Quinn said too quickly. 'But we don't do much of that nowadays. It's been some time since we had a good game, right, Ben?'

Driscoll gave him a scouring look, but followed it with a tight grin. 'Oh, we get a game in now and then. Well, I'll let you boys get at them steaks,' he said, rising from the table. 'Maynard, you can bring me a pot of coffee to take with me. And I'll be seeing you boys around.'

'Good to meet up with you,' O'Brien said without looking up.

When he was gone, and Quinn was back in the kitchen, Smith looked over his shoulder between bites and leaned forward toward O'Brien. 'Well, that was weird. I never thought you'd ask him to set with us.'

'It gave you a chance to downplay you hiring me,' O'Brien said. 'And for me to figure out what kind of bird he

is. I figure him as fast but not a good shot. He puts importance on speed, like a lot of gunfighters. But Wylie, on the
other hand, wears a Webley .45. It's accurate and hard-
hitting. If they all drew down out there, I'd take Wylie out
first. I see Latimer as the shoot-and-run type, and I doubt
Quinn ever killed a man.'

Smith was impressed. 'I guess it paid to set with him.'

'Maybe we'll find out tomorrow,' O'Brien suggested.

'Yeah,' Smith said in an unusually quiet voice.
'Tomorrow.'

That night was a long one. O'Brien spent the first part of it
cleaning the Winchester and Schofield, and loading his
gunbelt with cartridges. Then he lay awake for another sub-
stantial part of it, running over in his head what he and
Smith had planned. A few passengers were scheduled to
ride out on the Tulsa run from Fort Revenge, and he would
be among them. It was an early morning departure, and
they hoped Driscoll wouldn't be watching it; it would be
better if O'Brien's presence on the return trip were a surprise to them.

The morning was balmy and dry. The sun came up in an
explosion of color, striping the eastern sky with ribbons of
pastels. O'Brien had been up in the dark, even before
Smith, and was out on the porch of the depot to watch the
sunrise, and to look around for any Driscoll spies. He saw
nobody. In another half hour passengers began arriving,
and when Joe Reece called them out, O'Brien slipped in
among them and boarded the coach. By 8 a.m., with
Driscoll just waking up out at his cabin, the stagecoach left
the station, with Shanghai Smith looking after it solemnly,
wishing he were aboard.

The ride to Tulsa took most of the morning, and the

rough trail caused O'Brien's back to hurt again. Passengers tried unsuccessfully to engage him in conversation. The driver Joe Reece took O'Brien's Winchester up on the box with him, and O'Brien kept his revolver stuffed in his waist under his rawhides, out of sight.

Tulsa was a much bigger town than Fort Revenge, and was bustling with carriage and pedestrian traffic. Smith had rented depot space near the town's center, among stores and banks. The passengers who were to take passage back to Fort Revenge or farther were very upset when the driver, Reece, advised them they would have to take the next stage. One middle-aged man threatened to sue Smith. But then Reece was driving down the main street to the Tulsa Bank, and stopping out front. Two bank guards met them there, and helped load two boxes of gold and silver aboard. Then a bank vice-president came out on the street to speak with Reece.

'The president didn't want to use your line for payroll, after you had that hold-up recently,' the bespectacled fellow frowned. 'I told him it would be safe because you put a second man on the box. Don't let me down, Reece.'

Reece nodded. He was bulky, and bald under his hat, but he was good with his gun. He wore a Smith & Wesson revolver much like the one Corey McGraw had used to try to kill O'Brien.

'We're prepared for trouble, Mr Mason. This here is O'Brien, our man riding shotgun on this trip. We'll take good care of that payroll.'

Mason looked O'Brien over diffidently, noting that he had retrieved a rifle from the box of the coach and held it loosely under his arm now. 'I don't see a shotgun anywhere,' he said with an imperious frown. 'And I didn't know Smith was hiring backwoods Billies to take on serious work for him.'

O'Brien cocked the rifle, sliding a cartridge into the chamber, and planted the muzzle of the gun snugly against Mason's belly.

Mason's face went white.

'Now, do you feel any safer with me on the other end of this Winchester than you would if Reece here held an eight-gauge on you?' he asked in a low, hard voice.

Mason's mouth had gone old-paper dry. 'Take that gun off me!' he demanded in a cracking voice.

O'Brien dropped the muzzle of the gun. 'Just making a point, Mr Banker. Maybe you better stick to adding up accounts and leave the heavy stuff to them that knows it.'

'This is outrageous!' Mason fumed, eyeing O'Brien warily.

Reece was embarrassed. 'O'Brien don't mean no disrespect, Mr Mason. It's just his way. Shanghai Smith can't say enough praise about him. He's a wizard with that rifle.'

He turned to assess O'Brien's reaction to those remarks, but O'Brien was already climbing on to the seat of the coach. 'Come on, Reece. We got trail to cover.'

Reece gave Mason a sheepish grin, and climbed aboard to head out on what was potentially a very dangerous run.

Ben Driscoll had met with his three gang members about mid-morning, and finalized their plans to rob Smith's stagecoach when it arrived back from Tulsa late that day. They were all tense about the job ahead of them. O'Brien's arrival in town put a whole new look on everything. Driscoll wasn't at all convinced that O'Brien wouldn't be on that stage when it passed the old cavalry fort, despite Smith's pronouncements to the contrary, and that would make the operation more dangerous. He could count on Wylie in a shoot-out, but Latimer wasn't all that good with a gun, and

Quinn was practically worthless.

Not long after noon, to break the tension, Driscoll took Wylie into town to the general store there, just to look around, making the time pass. At about the same time, Emmet Purcell rode into town with his hired gun, Duke Hawley.

Both men were weary and sore from the long ride down to Fort Revenge, and the hardship camps on the trail. They were in a foul mood, especially Hawley, whose nerves had been scraped raw by his riding and camping with Purcell, who wasn't the easiest man to be with under these circumstances. Purcell always wanted to ride farther than Hawley thought necessary, and expected Hawley, his employee, to do all the work at camp.

Hawley had been an assistant to the now-deceased Corey McGraw back at the Purcell ranch, and gave off the heavy and dirty work to other hands. And before coming to Purcell, he had made his living gambling, and with his gun. He was lightning fast with his Starr .44, and had no hesitancy in using it.

The two of them reined in at the saloon, and looked around. 'Another one-horse town,' Purcell commented heavily, removing his hat and wiping at his sunburnt, square face and showing his gray hair.

Hawley grunted. He was dressed entirely in black, with silver medallions sewn on to his hat-band and along his trouser legs, in the Texas style – nobody ever took him for a ranch-hand. 'I've seen better-looking pigsties. Do you think he's still here?'

'Well, one of my contacts confirmed there's a stage line here run by a man that used to hunt buffalo. This man O'Brien probably knows him, and that might have kept him here.'

'Let's go talk to him.'

'No, no. If he's here today, he'll be here tomorrow. This man is dangerous, and we have to go carefully.'

'No offense, Emmet. But I eat boys like that for break-fast,' Hawley said arrogantly.

Purcell grinned. 'I know. That's why you're down here with me. But we'll find accommodation for the night right now, and I also want to buy myself a saddle-blanket. Mine is plumb wore out and chafing my mount. I see a store across the street there. Let's take a look.'

They dismounted and hitched their mounts to a rail. Hawley tightened the cinches on his saddle, and Purcell touched his horse's muzzle. 'It's OK, boy. You'll be bedded down before you know it.'

When the two men walked into the store, the proprietor was behind a long counter, talking to Ben Driscoll. There were shelves of dry goods and other items on the wall behind him, and bins of grain lined an end wall. A pickle barrel stood near the door.

Driscoll looked up at the newcomers, but One-Eye Wylie was studying some boxes of cartridges in a case at the back of the store. Purcell looked the place over with obvious dis-taste.

'Afternoon, gentlemen,' the owner greeted them. 'Be with you in just a minute.'

The two men walked over to the counter, and Purcell looked past the owner to a wool saddle-blanket on a nearby shelf. He glanced at Hawley, and nodded toward it. 'That will fit the bill,' he said.

Down the counter, Driscoll was about finished with the owner, and was very interested in the strangers. 'Go ahead, Williams,' he said to the owner. 'I'll think about that holster.'

'Is this the best you can do on these .45 cartridges?' Wylie called out to the owner.

'That's just barely over cost,' the owner called back. Then he turned to Purcell. 'Yes, sir?'

Purcell pointed at the saddle-blanket. 'How much is that blanket back there? And don't try to cheat me. I know prices.'

The owner gave him a sober look. 'I reckon you're new in town, mister. All prices in here are marked for a fair profit, and nothing more. That's two dollars.'

'Two dollars? That's highway robbery, but I'll have to take it.' He reached for a money pouch at his waist.

'That blanket is spoken for,' Ben Driscoll said in a low, even tone.

Purcell, Hawley and Wylie all turned to stare at him.

'That's right. I just asked this man to put it aside for me.' That was the truth, he needed a blanket, too.

Purcell looked irritated. 'Well, then give me a blanket just like that one.' To the owner.

The owner was looking a little tense. 'That one is the only one in stock, mister. There'll be some more in next week, if you can wait.'

'No, I can't wait!' Purcell frowned. 'What kind of a place you running here?'

Hawley stepped forward easily. 'Did this man pay you anything for the blanket?' he said in a quiet voice.

Driscoll squinted his hard eyes down on him.

'Why, not yet. But I made a deal with him,' the owner explained.

'There's no deal till money exchanges hands,' Hawley persisted. 'You can sell that blanket to this man.'

The owner looked scared. 'I don't know, gentlemen.'

'I know,' Driscoll grated out. 'I told you, mister. That

128

blanket is mine. Now maybe you ought to take your business someplace else.'

'Yeah. Someplace else,' Wylie said from the rear of the store. Then he went back to examining the box of cartridges.

Hawley had had enough. He squared away with Driscoll. 'Maybe you'd like to make us leave,' he said in a half-whisper.

'Maybe I would,' Driscoll replied in a chilling voice.

'Hawley,' Purcell warned him, remembering why they had come all this distance.

But it had gone beyond dissuasion now.

'Then make your move,' Hawley said almost inaudibly.

Wylie had finally turned away from his potential purchase, but still didn't see any danger to Driscoll. He now watched with growing interest as the two men dropped their hands to their guns. Driscoll was confident: he had never been beaten in a draw-down. With a half-smile on his lips, he suddenly drew the Remington .44 on his hip, intending to kill the arrogant stranger.

But by the time his revolver had cleared leather, Hawley's was out and firing. His Starr barked out loudly in the big room, and the slug hit Driscoll just below the heart. Driscoll still tried to aim and fire, but his shot went wild as Hawley put a second bullet in him, in the high chest.

Driscoll, not realizing yet what had happened to him, went staggering backwards and slammed into a bin of corn seed there, cracking the bin and making the seed pour on to the floor. He ended up sitting in front of the bin, staring into space, eyes open but in the rictus of death.

Wylie was wide-eyed. 'Why, you—' He began a draw, but found Hawley's Starr trained on him.

'Go ahead,' Hawley told him. 'You can join your Maker with your friend there.'

129

Wylie hesitated, then took his hand away from his gun. 'You killed him! You killed Ben Driscoll!'

'Was that his name?' Hawley said drily. 'Now, get on out of here, bug-eye. It makes me sick looking at you.'

Wylie came past him, giving him a fierce look. 'This ain't over, stranger. That man's got friends here in town. I'd advise you to watch your back.'

'I always do when I'm around vermin like you,' Hawley replied.

By mid-afternoon O'Brien and Reece were halfway to Fort Revenge, and without incident. Reece thought that was a good sign.

Dust was kicking up all around them, and they both were wearing kerchiefs over their faces, which made it difficult to communicate.

'They might of backed off, thinking there might be two of us,' Reece commented from behind the cloth. The coach bucked and swayed over the rough trail.

O'Brien glanced over at him. 'They won't back off permanent,' he said. 'So it's better if they go ahead and try for this payroll. Then it'll be over, one way or the other. Anyway, if they hit us, it will be down toward Fort Revenge. There's a couple of areas of rocks to hide in. And the old fort. We drive right past it.'

'Well, I for one hope they give it up today. I ain't eager for no show-down with four armed men.'

O'Brien was disgruntled with him. 'Just be ready if we see them,' he told Reece. 'Follow my lead. And don't throw your gun down no matter what.'

Reece sighed behind the kerchief. 'I'll just be glad to get to Scobeyville.'

The news that a stranger had killed Ben Driscoll rippled

130

through Fort Revenge like a ground tremor. Purcell bought the saddle-blanket, but he was angry with Hawley. He knew they didn't need attention drawn to them so soon, when their reason for being there was to find O'Brien.

The store owner certified to Mayor Spencer that the shooting was lawful, since Driscoll had drawn on Hawley. By late afternoon Driscoll was in the hands of the mortician, and Wylie had reported to Quinn and Latimer what had happened.

'Well, that's it!' Quinn said excitedly. 'Ben was the heart of this. And who knows? Smith might have hired this stranger to take us all out, one by one!'

'If that was the case, he'd have tried to kill me,' Wylie said sourly. 'This don't change nothing for me. I say we go on and do the job.'

Latimer nodded. 'I can go along with that. It's still Ben's plan, and it's a good one.'

'Well, count me out,' Quinn said decisively. 'And if you're still going to try it, I'm getting out of town for a while.'

They were at Latimer's old house. Wylie regarded Quinn with disdain. 'Ben never should of brought you in. You ain't no good at all. Go on, get out. We don't need you, fry cook.'

Quinn left moments later, and when he was gone, Wylie turned to Latimer. 'OK. It's just you and me. And we're changing Ben's plan.'

Latimer furrowed his dark brow. 'Changing it?'

'That's right. I suddenly got an idea that will make it all work. And that Carter woman will work right into it.'

'Sarah? You're talking crazy, Wylie.'

'That woman spit in your face, Latimer. She won't never be anything to you, you know that. She owes you, don't she?'

Latimer shook his head. 'I ain't through with that one.

131

That hunter won't be around to protect her after today. We got unfinished business.'

'That's just it. But I got an idea she can be some use right now. In my changed plan for that stage job.'

'I don't get it, Wylie.'

Wylie grinned a crooked, one-eye grin at him. 'Just hear me out,' he said. 'I think you'll like it.'

CHAPTER TWELVE

It was getting to be late afternoon. Emmet Purcell and Hawley found their way down to Shanghai Smith's Territorial Express depot and identified themselves as friends of O'Brien from Montana. Purcell's smooth manner convinced Smith, and he admitted to O'Brien's presence there. He advised them that O'Brien was out on a run for him, and probably wouldn't be available to meet anybody until the following day. He referred them to Mrs Barstow's rooming house, and Purcell left, satisfied that his hunt for the buffalo hunter would soon be over.

Smith heard about the Driscoll shooting after they left, but didn't suspect he had spoken to Driscoll's killer when the two were there. He was shocked by the news, and figured rightly that this would change the gang's plans. Even if they persisted without Driscoll, they might wait until a better time.

At Mrs Barstow's place, Sarah Carter was going over some of Smith's accounts, checking his figures for him, when she heard the news. She had only seen Driscoll on the street, and had no feelings about his demise except to mentally note that he had been a friend of Jake Latimer. In late afternoon she saw Purcell and Hawley being shown to a room by

Mrs Barstow, but had no idea they had been involved in the shooting of Driscoll. Down the street from there, Wylie and Latimer were riding toward the Barstow house, with new plans about a hold-up that was still on their agenda for that day.

O'Brien and Reece were getting close to town. They figured when they got there, if it was without incident, they would make a quick stop to refresh the team, then drive on to Scobeyville to deliver the payroll there.

Now they were passing the old fort, built by the cavalry just after the Civil War to defend homesteaders and ranchers from attacks by Mescaleros and Comanches. The town's namesake was in total ruin, the stockade walls falling down, and the compound inhabited by prairie dogs.

As they approached the fort, O'Brien was very watchful. This was, he knew, an excellent spot for an ambush. Because he was hoping for a showdown, he had Reece slow the stage somewhat as they passed the site. But then they were past it, and heading on into Fort Revenge.

O'Brien pulled his kerchief down, and turned to Reece as they bumped along. 'This is mighty strange,' he said. 'We're almost back. It looks like they decided to pass this one up. Unless they're going to hit us between Fort Revenge and Scobeyville.'

'I'm just glad to get this far without any shooting,' Reece said, pulling his kerchief down, too. They were both dust-covered.

'Well, we're not at Scobeyville yet,' O'Brien said. 'Just remember what I been telling you.'

Reece made a face. 'I got it,' he said sourly.

Within fifteen minutes they were driving into Fort Revenge, and O'Brien reluctantly concluded that there would be no confrontation that day. He laid the Winchester

134

down beside him on the seat, to stretch his arms.

But there had been big developments in town. Wylie had forced Maynard Quinn to go to Sarah at the Barstow place, and lure her to Smith's depot by telling her that Smith wanted to speak with her, and it was about O'Brien. The message had the desired effect, and Sarah rushed to the depot, only to find Wylie and Latimer there, and Smith and one of his drivers bound and gagged in the reception area. Potential passengers had been previously advised that the stage from Tulsa would be taking none on this run, so the depot was otherwise entirely empty.

Sarah came in from the street and looked around the room. She gasped when she saw Smith and the other gagged man. 'What is this?' she said warily to Jake Latimer. He and Wylie were standing near the doorway.

'What is it?' Latimer grinned. 'It's the real world, missy.' He drew his Colt .44 and walked over to her, and placed its muzzle against her forehead. 'Now you're going to do just what we tell you. Understand?'

She gasped again. Over on a long bench for waiting passengers, sitting near his driver, Smith made muffled noises under the gag, and struggled against the ropes that bound him.

Latimer dropped the gun to his side, and Wylie came over very close to her. 'If you don't do exactly what we say, these men die. If you give us any trouble when the stage arrives, your friend O'Brien dies. Get it?'

'Oh, no,' Sarah moaned. Wylie went behind her, and pulled her hands back there to tie them up, as she flinched under his handling.

She looked over at Latimer. 'You animal. To think that I had serious thoughts of marrying you.'

'Hey, don't complain. You had a chance for a good thing.

135

But your buffalo man got in the way. Now you can be of some use, anyway.'

Wylie turned toward the street. 'I hear it. They're almost here.'

As Reece drove up to stop in front of the depot, O'Brien was surprised not to see Shanghai Smith standing out front looking for them. They pulled up in a cloud of dust, as O'Brien retrieved the Winchester from the seat beside him. Reece started to climb down, but O'Brien put a hand on his arm.

'Wait. There's something wrong here.'

'What?'

'Where's Smitty?' O'Brien wondered. 'Draw your piece.'

Reece frowned. 'What for?'

'Just do it,' O'Brien insisted.

Reece followed orders just as Sarah emerged on to the board porch, with Wylie nudging at her back. Latimer was beside him. They both had their guns drawn, and Wylie's was at Sarah's back.

'Well, you made it!' Wylie called out to them. 'Right on time!'

Reece's eyes narrowed down. 'Oh-oh.'

O'Brien was looking around quickly for Driscoll and Quinn.

'No, the others ain't here,' Wylie grinned. 'But we thought the woman would do just as good.'

'I'm sorry, O'Brien!' Sarah cried out.

'Where's Smitty?' O'Brien said.

'Oh, he's OK,' Wylie said. 'For now. We got him tied up inside. I reckon he's hoping everything goes all right out here.' A giggling laugh.

'All you got to do is throw your guns down,' Latimer told

136

them. 'That's how easy it all is. Then we'll tie you up like your boss, and drive the stage on out of here. Nobody will get hurt, and we'll have what we want – that payroll under the box.'

'They won't kill me, O'Brien!' Sarah called out again. 'Don't disarm yourselves!'

Wylie stepped forward. 'You see, O'Brien? The little woman don't know we're serious about all this. But you do, don't you?'

'Throw the guns down,' Latimer repeated. 'We ain't going to wait all day on this. We don't want bloodshed. We just want the loot.'

Reece spoke to O'Brien without taking his eyes off the gunmen. 'I guess we don't have much choice, O'Brien. I think they might kill her. Maybe they will leave without no shooting.'

O'Brien was shaking his head. He had never had a woman make him trouble a hundredth part of what Sarah Carter had in this brief time. 'Stand fast, Reece,' he said quietly. Then he called out the only thing he could think of. 'We ain't throwing down. Go ahead and kill the girl.'

Sarah's jaw dropped slightly open. Latimer and Wylie exchanged a dark look.

'Do you think we're bluffing here, buffalo man?' Wylie hissed out. He was hidden behind Sarah, except for his face. Latimer was using a support post for cover. Wylie cocked his Webley and shoved it against Sarah's temple. 'Throw them guns down now, or I put a hole in this lady's head!'

'As soon as we're disarmed, they'll kill us all,' O'Brien said quietly to Reece. 'Including Sarah and Smitty.' He called out to Wylie. 'Well, go ahead and kill her!' he said loudly. 'But then you'll be exposed, Wylie, and that works out real nice for us.'

Wylie hesitated. Latimer glanced over at him nervously. 'This ain't working.'

'You keep talking about it, and she'll probably faint on you,' O'Brien called out, looking Sarah in the eye and putting emphasis on the word, 'faint'. 'Better make up your mind, Wylie.'

Sarah saw O'Brien's eyes, and realized he was sending her a message. Wylie was holding her by her right arm, and she figured that if she feigned losing consciousness, and let her legs release her weight, she could fall away from him and he wouldn't be able to abort her fall.

'OK, if you want her dead, she's dead!' Wylie shouted angrily.

'Wylie, wait!' Latimer called over. He wanted time to think this through. Once the girl was gone, it was a whole different situation.

Wylie looked over at him for just a moment, and in that moment, Sarah made a gasping sound in her throat and collapsed out of his grasp. He tried to catch her, but it wasn't possible. She hit the wood planks of the porch on her side, and Wylie found himself exposed to view.

There was a cracking explosion from O'Brien's Winchester, just as Wylie aimed his revolver to fire. O'Brien's shot caught Wylie in center chest, over the heart, and threw him back into the depot, where he hit the floor hard. His gun had fired off as he was hit, and O'Brien was struck under his left arm, in the ribs. Latimer had now fired off two shots at Reece, with one missing and the other punching him hard in the side. O'Brien swung the barrel of the rifle over toward Latimer while Wylie was still on his way inside, and pumped off two more shots, the rifle banging in Wylie's ears, and hit Latimer in the left arm and the face. The second shot killed him instantly, as he banged against the building wall and then slid to the boardwalk, a blue hole in his right cheek.

Reece had tumbled off the seat of the coach, and was lying in the dust beside a front wheel. Wylie was on his back inside, his eyes staring at the depot ceiling. His left leg drummed at the floor once, and then he was motionless.

As the gunsmoke cleared, there was an acrid odor of it in the air. O'Brien climbed off the coach stiffly, after the long ride there. Down the street, Purcell and Hawley had seen the whole thing at a distance, and now stepped back out of sight at a store entrance.

'That's him,' Purcell said in a whisper. 'The man in the rawhides. Did you see that?'

'I saw it,' Hawley said without inflection. He wasn't impressed.

At the depot, O'Brien was bending over Reece as Sarah got to her feet. Reece was bleeding, but the wound looked pretty good. He helped Reece to his feet, ignoring his own flesh wound at his rib cage. 'You'll be OK,' he said. 'We'll get you down to the vet.'

Reece made it inside on his own, as O'Brien stopped beside Sarah. 'Glad you got my message,' he said with a grin.

'I knew you wouldn't let them kill me,' she said, tears in her eyes.

'You played it real smart,' he told her. 'You saved yourself.'

Under an unexpected impulse, she came and threw her arms around his broad shoulders. 'I'm so glad you're safe!' Her cheeks were damp with tears. Once again, O'Brien was caught by surprise. He hesitated, then put a hand on her waist. He decided it felt good there.

'It's OK, Sarah,' he said quietly.

139

'There I go again. I'm sorry.' She pulled away from him.

'I liked it,' he said.

She stared into his eyes, emotions running through her wildly. 'I'll go take a look at Reece,' she said softly.

A moment later O'Brien was taking the gags off Smith and his driver while Sarah examined Reece's wound.

'You did it!' Smith was exclaiming as O'Brien untied him. 'I figured you could take them!'

'We was lucky. There was only two,' O'Brien said.

'Ben Driscoll was shot down at the general store by a stranger in town,' Smith explained. 'I reckon that scared Quinn off?'

'A stranger?' O'Brien said.

'I don't know how it happened. There was people in town looking for you, too. I sent them over to Barstow's. Said they was your friends. From Montana.'

Sarah looked over at them. 'It was one of those you sent over that killed Driscoll,' she said. 'It's all over town.'

O'Brien and Smith exchanged a look. 'I ain't got no friends in Montana,' he said to Smith. 'What did they look like, Smitty?'

Smith shrugged. He and his driver were unbound now, and rubbing their wrists. Reece had lain down on a depot bench. His side wound was a shallow one, but he was feeling faint. Sarah had sat down with him, trying to avoid looking at Wylie's inert form on the floor. O'Brien and Smith acted as if he wasn't there. O'Brien's wound under his arm was just a grazing hit, and there was little blood. He had already forgotten he was shot.

'One was an older man,' Smith was saying. 'The one with him looked like a gunfighter.'

'That sounds like Purcell, here with a hired gun,' O'Brien told him.

140

'The rancher that sent them boys after you?'

O'Brien nodded. 'Looks like he ain't quit yet.'

Sarah had been listening. 'Oh, heavens. Does it ever end?'

O'Brien took a deep breath in, and glanced toward the corpse of Wylie a short distance away, and at the leg of the dead Latimer that just showed beyond the doorway. He had seen Sarah close her eyes against Latimer's violent death.

'Oh, it will end, Sarah,' he said tiredly, retrieving his rifle from the bench beside Smith. 'It will end right soon. That much you can count on.'

CHAPTER THIRTEEN

Within a half hour of the depot confrontation, Reece was at the veterinarian's house, with his wound being treated. O'Brien refused any assistance, making his own small bandage. The only pain from his wound was a dull burning, but the previous one in his back was still limiting his range of motion.

One-Eye Wylie and Jake Latimer were delivered to the mortician, and joined Ben Driscoll there. They would all be buried the next day, before the corpses began to smell up the funeral home. Maynard Quinn had hung a closed sign on his restaurant and ridden out of town right after luring Sarah down to the stage depot.

O'Brien was frustrated. Smith had promised to pay him off the following day, so O'Brien would have his grubstake for his trip south. But now there were a couple of complications: Sarah Carter and Emmet Purcell.

Sarah was a new experience for him. He had never formed a serious relationship with any woman, and had never expected to. But the way this one looked at him seemed to soften something inside him, maybe partially removed the hard grip on his insides that life on the hardship trail had put there – at least when he was in her presence. He knew he had to address this before he could just ride off. And he had no idea how.

Emmet Purcell was a different problem. It seemed pretty clear he wasn't going to quit until he had avenged his son's death at O'Brien's hands, and O'Brien couldn't leave town without resolving that. He had never run from trouble in his life, and never would.

Sarah had recovered from her ordeal outside the depot. She had just minor bruises from her fall, and she felt much calmer. She wanted to tend O'Brien's shallow wound, but he told her to go back to Barstow's to clean up and rest.

Smith sent the stage on to Scobeyville with the driver who had been tied up with him, then went back to the bunkhouse area of the depot building to get a report on the Tulsa run from O'Brien while the hunter cleaned up at an old wash bowl.

'Somebody said Quinn rode out before the shoot-out,' he told O'Brien as his friend toweled off. His shaggy hair was wild-looking; there was a blue mark on his side where Wylie's slug had grazed him, and some dried blood. Smith gave him some tape and gauze, and O'Brien applied the small bandage and pulled his rawhide shirt on. As he yanked a big comb through his thick, graying hair, Smith leaned against the nearby wall.

'I don't know how you do it. You look like you just come off an aspen-shaded picnic.'

O'Brien gave him a small grin, a rarity for him. 'This beats busting every rise on your belly like a snake, eating buffalo dust, getting smeared with buffalo dung. Trying to keep from being tore up under their hoofs when they run.'

Smith returned the grin. 'Them was the good days,' he said. He looked down at the floor. 'You don't have to do

143

this, you know.'

O'Brien looked over at him. His hair was slicked back, his beard was combed, and he looked almost civilized.

'You don't have to meet Purcell. Where you're going, he'd never find you. I'll pay you off when I open the safe tomorrow, and you can just ride out.'

O'Brien held his gaze with a sober one. 'No. I can't.'

Smith sighed. 'I knew that. Just thought I'd try.' He pushed his big bulk off the wall. 'I guess it wouldn't do any good to ask if I could be with you.'

'No, it wouldn't.'

Smith nodded disconsolately. 'Well. I guess I'll walk on down to Quinn's place and make sure that low-life really left town.'

O'Brien nodded. 'Be careful,' he told him.

Smith left then and walked toward town. The sun was lowering in the western sky, and there was a peaceful feeling in the streets. Smith walked down to the Quinn café, and was surprised to see lights on inside despite the closed sign on the door. Then the door opened and Purcell and Hawley emerged.

'Mr Smith!' Purcell said, smiling. 'Glad to see you still alive! I hear you had some real trouble down at the depot earlier.'

'Mr Brown,' Smith responded. 'Yes, we had ourselfs a little set-to down there. The boys that made the trouble are at the mortuary now. Is the restaurant open?'

'I reckon not,' Purcell said. 'We saw lights and went in, but there's nobody there. Pretty strange, don't you think?'

'I think Mr Quinn left town in a hurry,' Smith said. 'I guess he didn't turn the kerosene down.'

Hawley was standing there through the dialogue, studying Smith with a half-grin on his narrow, bony face. His

144

Starr .44 hung menacingly at his side.

'I hear our mutual friend O'Brien handled himself pretty well,' Purcell went on. 'Is he staying with you at the depot then? We'll want to say hello tomorrow morning before we leave town.'

Smith took a deep breath in. 'Maybe we ought to talk about O'Brien, Mr Brown. Private-like. Why don't we step back into the restaurant? I'm sure Mr Quinn won't mind. I could fix us some coffee.'

Purcell frowned slightly, then nodded. 'All right. I have a few minutes.' He turned to Hawley. 'I'll see you back at the house, Jones.'

Hawley frowned heavily. 'Are you sure?'

Purcell forced a smile. 'Absolutely. I won't be long at all.'

Hawley turned reluctantly and left them, and Smith re-opened the cafe door for them and they went in. Purcell seated himself at a table, and Smith went into the kitchen to heat up some coffee while Purcell waited impatiently. When Smith re-emerged with two cups of coffee and placed them on the table, he grinned down at Purcell.

'Now, Mr Brown,' he said. 'Let's talk.'

Sarah had cleaned up and changed into other clothes in her room at Mrs Barstow's, and shortly after Hawley's arrival back there, she left again to walk down to the stage depot. She had so much to discuss with O'Brien that she was reluctant to wait until morning. Things were happening very fast in Fort Revenge now, and circumstances were changing all the time.

She passed Quinn's restaurant just as Smith was sitting down to talk with Purcell, but didn't look inside to see who was there. A few minutes later she was at the depot, and walking to the rear where she found O'Brien. He was alone back there, sitting on a lower bunk, cleaning his Winchester rifle. He looked up in surprise when she came in.

'Sarah! I thought you'd be resting up from that fracas here.'

She came and sat on a bunk across from him. It was getting dark outside, and he had turned up several lamps, but the light was soft, and made Sarah look particularly pretty. 'I wanted to talk with you.'

He laid the rifle across his knees. 'I'm kind of busy right now, Sarah. But I'll stop past Mrs Barstow's tomorrow morning, and we'll have more time.'

He ran a cloth over the barrel of the rifle, and laid it aside. Then he picked up his Schofield revolver from the bunk beside him. He broke it open and peered through the barrel.

'Mayor Spencer found out I was helping Mr Smith with his accounts, and offered me a job,' she said.

He looked up and smiled. 'That's just fine, Sarah.'

'He says the town needs a treasurer, and I can have the position. It doesn't pay much, but it will support me at Mrs Barstow's. I won't have to return to Boston.'

O'Brien was very pleased. 'I'm glad. I expect you would-n't take to that life now, after what you been through out here.'

'I wish you were staying on. I know Mr Smith offered you a permanent job.'

He sighed softly. 'We been through this, Sarah. I ain't got all the trail punched out of me yet.' But seeing her sitting there across from him, looking so lovely in that soft light, he felt something inside him responding to Sarah in a way that made him oddly uncomfortable. He tried to shove the thing down inside him, where he wouldn't take notice of it, but it didn't work. He stuffed the Schofield into his belt and

146

picked up the rifle.

'I shouldn't be talking like this. I wouldn't, back in Boston. I guess it's what the frontier has done to me. But I have to tell you this, O'Brien. I've grown very fond of you.'

He had looked bears and cougars in the eye without flinching. But when he glanced over at Sarah now, it was with trepidation. This was all new to him, and unsettling. 'Likewise, Sarah.'

Her face lightened up as if a morning sun had struck it. She tried to keep tears from her eyes. 'Oh, dear.'

He rose quickly from the bunk, holding the rifle. 'I got business now. It might get a mite risky for you up at the other end of town, so I want you to stay here till I get back.'

She really noticed his two guns for the first time. 'Those men. The ones that came after you here.'

'I can't turn my back on it, Sarah. It has to play out.'

'You can ask Spencer to take some men and arrest them until a federal marshal arrives. One will be back here soon.'

O'Brien shook his head at that idea. 'And I'm sure they'd just turn their guns over and go with him peacefully.'

She made a face, and he thought even that was pretty. 'Oh, I know I sound silly. But there must be some way out of this.'

'No, Sarah. There isn't.'

'So what do you intend to do when you find them?'

He regarded her quizzically. 'Why, I reckon I'll have to kill them.'

A little shudder passed through her. 'Or they'll kill you.'

'You just stay put here, Sarah. I'll be back later. When it's over.'

She reached up and placed a soft kiss on his cheek, and then blushed. 'I had to do that. Just in case.'

He stood there and stared at her, and something stirred

147

inside his chest. His mouth went dry, and that had never happened before. 'Maybe I better get on out of here. Remember. Stay put.'

'I will, O'Brien,' she said, a heavy lump in her throat. 'I will.'

Up the street, at Quinn's re-opened restaurant, Shanghai Smith and Emmet Purcell were sipping their coffee.

'Let's get down to brass tacks, Mr Brown,' Smith was saying to him. 'I know who you really are.'

'Oh?'

'You're Emmet Purcell, and you come here to kill O'Brien.'

Purcell started to object, but decided otherwise. 'OK. You got me. And now that you know, you can tell that murdering friend of yours that we're calling him out. Me and Hawley. He has to pay for what he did.'

'I guess he killed your son.'

Purcell looked past him, remembering. 'That's right. Tully was just trying to take a couple of rustlers into custody, and this O'Brien knifed him when he wasn't looking. He also killed one of my ranch-hands that was with Tully, and a second one barely escaped.'

'That ain't the way he told it,' Smith said. 'He said your son shot his riding partner at long distance, trying out a new Sharps rifle. Then he was going to hang O'Brien to the nearest tree.'

'Hanging would be too good for him,' Purcell said darkly.

'The thing is, Mr Purcell,' Smith went on, 'I known O'Brien almost since he come out here from the East. And I never known him to cheat another man, or lie or steal. He just ain't got it in him. It's a code he lives by.'

Purcell remembered Wade Lucas telling him that O'Brien and his partner probably weren't the rustlers they were watching for. But he hadn't wanted to hear any talk like that.

'Well, I reckon that's your story. I see it different.'

Smith leaned forward on his chair. 'I'd bet my life that O'Brien never stole your cattle, Mr Purcell. And I wouldn't defend him if he had. You can ask anybody that knows me. I wouldn't lie for him.'

Purcell studied Smith's beefy face. 'You could be wrong.'

Smith nodded. 'That's always possible. But it ain't likely. A man don't change his colors overnight and become a thief. Think that over, Mr Purcell. And while you're doing that, think of this, too. In thirty years of face-downs with drifters and Indians, nobody never took O'Brien down. Your man Hawley might get the first shot in. But then O'Brien will kill him. And you.'

Purcell narrowed his eyes down on Smith, and just sat there absorbing that. Remembering that O'Brien had already killed Corey McGraw. If he managed to kill Hawley, Purcell would be left without a decent foreman to run his ranch.

Smith hefted his enormous bulk off his chair, and took a last sip of coffee. 'If you want to take that kind of risk to try to kill an innocent man, just because he defended himself against your son, Mr Purcell, well, I guess I can't stop you. But I think it's about time you used some judgment in this thing. Think it over.'

At that moment, O'Brien passed the restaurant and looked in. He was surprised to see Smith there with the man that was obviously Purcell. Thinking Smith was just trying to separate Purcell from his gunman, and suspecting Hawley was at the Barstow place, he walked on up there to confront him; he would deal with Purcell later.

When O'Brien walked into the boarding house, he found Hawley immediately. He had just paid Mrs Barstow for the night's lodging, and she was giving him a receipt. When O'Brien came into the big parlor that served as a reception area, Hawley turned and saw him at once.

'Well, I'll be,' Hawley grinned. 'The buffalo man.'

'I thought you might be looking for me,' O'Brien said. He held the Winchester at ready in his right hand; the Schofield was still tucked into his belt at his waist.

'I see you came prepared for bear,' Hawley suggested. 'You think any of that firepower will help you now, dung picker?'

Mrs Barstow and a middle-aged male resident quickly exited the room, and left the two alone.

'I reckon we're about to find out,' O'Brien told him.

Hawley had no fear of the hunter. He had never lost in a draw-down in his life, and could draw so fast the eye couldn't follow. He squared away with O'Brien, his hand out over the Starr revolver that had killed so easily before. 'Take a good look at me, mister. I'm the last thing you'll ever see.'

O'Brien carefully took the rifle into both hands. 'You aim to talk me to death, or actually use that sidearm?' he said in a low, even tone.

But at that very moment, Emmet Purcell came through the open doorway. 'Hold it, Hawley!' he called out.

O'Brien swung his head around, and saw that Purcell hadn't drawn his gun. Also, Smith was standing just behind Purcell. He turned back to Hawley.

Hawley was frowning at his boss. 'What for? This is what we come for, Emmet,' he said, in a low, hoarse tone. Then he went for his gun in a flashing movement.

When he cleared the holster, though, O'Brien's rifle was

aimed at his heart.

Neither man fired.

'What's the matter, big man?' O'Brien growled out. 'Afraid to die?'

'I said, hold it, Hawley!' Purcell cried out again. He and Smith were both inside the room now, and Smith's fat-crowded eyes were big.

Hawley stood there assessing the situation. Then, after a moment that seemed an eternity, he holstered the Starr. O'Brien slowly lowered the rifle, then turned toward Purcell, just as confused as Hawley.

'What's the matter with you, Emmet?' Hawley said loudly. 'This man killed your son! He murdered Tully!'

Purcell sighed. He went over and put a hand on Hawley's shoulder. 'I found out some things from this man here. And I believe him. This hunter didn't rustle none of my cattle. Tully got the wrong people.'

'How do you know that?' Hawley argued. But inside him, he was secretly glad he hadn't drawn O'Brien's fire. 'They could both be lying to you.'

'Well, if they are, that's something I'm going to have to live with,' Purcell told him. 'But the killing is done with, Hawley. Go get our things. I think we can reach Sulphur Creek tonight. I don't want to spend even one night here now.'

Hawley let a long breath out. 'OK, Emmet. It's your show.' He gave O'Brien a last dark look, and went off to their room.

Purcell turned then to O'Brien. 'I got an apology to make, I guess. I went crazy when you killed Tully. But, looking into your eyes now, I can see you ain't no rustler. Tully made a mistake. He was always a rash boy.'

O'Brien nodded. 'I'm real sorry about your boy, Purcell.

But he wasn't in no mood to listen to my story. It's just too bad all around.'

Smith was grinning now. 'You done the right thing, Mr Purcell. There's been enough bloodshed over this.'

Purcell nodded. Seeing O'Brien up close, he was sure he would have killed Hawley. 'We'll be gone within the hour. And thank you, Mr Smith.'

'I was just telling the truth,' Smith told him. 'Just the truth.'

CHAPTER
FOURTEEN

Sarah was so relieved to see O'Brien back at the depot alive and unhurt that she cried uncontrollably for several minutes. O'Brien didn't know how to react to that, or what to do, but Smith comforted her until she got herself under control.

'You better get yourself back to Barstow's now,' O'Brien told her then, awkwardly. 'Smitty, would you mind walking her back there?'

Sarah was surprised and a little hurt that O'Brien hadn't volunteered to do that himself. She felt very close to him, but it was like he was pushing her away, wanting to distance himself from her.

'Oh, sure,' Smith said, eyeing O'Brien sidewise. 'I'll see that the lady gets back safe and sound.'

'I got to go check on the Appaloosa,' O'Brien said then. 'I'll be riding out tomorrow.'

Smith peeked a look at Sarah, to see her reaction to that. 'Yeah, that's right,' he said quietly. 'I'll be paying you off soon as I open up tomorrow.'

Sarah turned to O'Brien. 'Will I see you before you leave?' she said.

He looked over at her. 'I'll be here at the depot till Smitty opens up and we meet with the mayor. I can stop past Mrs Barstow's after that.'

'I think I'd rather walk down here, if that's all right,' she said.

O'Brien nodded to her. 'Of course, Sarah. I reckon I owe you a talk, anyway.'

She wondered how she should take that. 'All right. I'll see both of you then. Let's go, Mr Smith,' she said soberly, with a weak smile. 'I'm ready.'

By the time O'Brien had returned from the hostelry, Smith had arrived back at the depot. He found O'Brien back at the rear, washing up. The Scobeyville coach had dusted in about mid-evening, and its driver was fast asleep in one of the bunks down a long aisle.

'I see Funk got back,' Smith observed. 'I reckon he got that payroll to Scobeyville OK.'

'Then it was a good day after all,' O'Brien remarked, drying his face with a towel. His rawhide shirt was beltless, and his stovepipe boots were sitting empty over by his bunk.

'Any day above ground is a good day,' Smith grinned at him.

O'Brien went over and sat on his bunk, and examined his Schofield. 'You must of done some fast talking in the restaurant. I wouldn't have thought Purcell could be talked down.'

'All he'd heard up to now was lies,' Smith said. 'And he wanted to believe them. You can't blame him.'

'I don't blame him. I blame his son.'

'When I was up at Barstow's, I heard them ride out,' Smith said. 'You won't hear from Purcell again.'

'I guess I should thank you.'

'It's that Hawley should thank me. He'd be down at the

mortuary now, with quarters on his eyes.' He came and sat down beside O'Brien.

O'Brien looked over at him. 'I appreciate this grubstake, Smitty.'

'Appreciate? You saved my company, partner! You saved this town from going down. The mayor thinks you're heaven-sent!'

'We all got lucky, I reckon.'

Smith looked over at him. 'You know I want you to stay on here, O'Brien.'

'Yes. I know.'

'You could come in as a partner. Invest your grubstake. You know how good we always worked together.'

'You're one of the few men I could trust,' O'Brien admitted.

'I don't like to say it, but you're getting up there, mister. When are you going to get tired of hauling beaver out of ice-cold water and stuffing down burned bear meat over a brush fire? That just ain't fit work for no mature man. You got to settle down some time.'

'It's all I know, Smitty. You know that. That's where I'm really alive. Out there in hardship camp, frying bacon on a mesquite stick. Hunting for fox and rabbits. Checking traps on a frosty morning. It's what I am, what I always have been.'

'What about the girl? I think she's took a hankering for you.'

O'Brien looked up quickly, defensively. 'I reckon Sarah is my business, Smitty.'

Smith arched his thick brows. 'Sorry. I just hoped you was taking her for what she is. She's the real thing, partner. I could tell it when I first met her.'

O'Brien regarded him with mild impatience. 'You usually listen better than this, you old hide scraper.'

'You're right, it ain't none of my business. But I never was good at keeping my big mouth shut. I'm going to think on this tonight. Maybe you wouldn't take it wrong if I talked to you about all this again tomorrow morning.'

O'Brien gave him a narrow look. 'I don't know how I'd go about stopping you.'

Sarah knew that Smith would open for business early the following day, so she had a quick breakfast and walked down to the depot shortly afterwards.

It was a beautiful April morning. A soft breeze brought the scent of wildflowers in off the plains, and the sun was rising majestically over a rise of distant hills. When she arrived at the depot and saw O'Brien's Appaloosa hitched up and saddled outside the building, along with a second horse, she felt a tightness in her stomach. When she went inside, O'Brien and Smith were seated in Smith's office off the waiting room, and Mayor Spencer was just leaving. No passengers had arrived yet.

'Oh, good morning, Sarah!' Spencer greeted her with a big smile. 'My new treasurer looks well on this fine Oklahoma day!'

'Good morning, Mr Mayor.'

'They're inside there.' He gave her a knowing look, and she had no idea what it meant. 'See you later.'

Spencer left, and Sarah went on into the small office.

'Oh, come on in, Sarah!' Smith said in his booming voice. 'We been expecting you!'

'I was afraid I might have missed you,' she said to O'Brien. She was a little breathless.

'No, ma'am,' O'Brien assured her. 'I wouldn't have left without seeing you.'

Smith had the same wide grin on his heavy features that

the mayor had exhibited. 'O'Brien and me been talking since before dawn,' he told her. 'We got some things settled that might interest you.'

O'Brien gave him a sour look, and Smith nodded and rose from his desk. 'Well. I'll let O'Brien fill you in. I'll just go get R.C. Funk out of bed. He's got a run coming up at mid-morning.'

When Smith had waddled off, O'Brien turned to Sarah. 'Sit down, Sarah. I wanted to talk with you some when you got here.'

Sarah frowned a pretty frown, and seated herself on a straight chair near him. She looked very good to him, in her lemon-hued gingham dress and dark hair down to her shoulders. 'What is it, O'Brien?'

He took a deep breath in. 'Well. Me and Smitty been talking up a storm here this morning. He got some ideas in his head last night, and told me about them while I saddled the Appaloosa. Then we talked some more in here, when him and the mayor was paying me off.'

She regarded him quizzically.

'Smitty made me an offer that kind of works in with what I been planning for myself. He said if I stay here and work with him, I could share in the profits of the business. I'd just have to make a little investment.'

'I see,' she said, her heart suddenly beating fast.

'I said no to that.'

She stopped breathing. 'Oh.'

'But then this morning we talked again. Smitty decided to go out trapping with me. There's supposed to be good country for that south of here. We'd work together, like we used to with buffalo. Then I'd come back with him to help run the stageline. He promised we'd do that a few times a year, till the trapping runs out. But we'd be here most of the

157

time. If I can take town living.'

Sarah could hardly believe what he was saying. Her heart was pummeling at her chest, and she felt a welling of raw emotion. 'Are you sure this is what you want? This is an important decision.'

He nodded awkwardly. 'I reckon so, Sarah.' Talking to a woman this way was all new to him. He was learning as he went along.

'Sarah, you and me been through some things together. Things that make me feel different about you than any woman I ever known. Like I said before, I like you. You took all you been through better than most women that lived their whole lives out here. That means something to me.'

She was fighting hard not to cry. 'That's nice of you to say.'

'Since I'll be in town most of the time now, I was thinking we might see each other once in a while. I mean, I could call for you at Mrs Barstow's. If you're of a mind.' He avoided meeting her eye through that long pronouncement.

Now her eyes went moist. She couldn't help it. 'I am of a mind,' she told him, her voice breaking slightly. 'I'd like that very much, O'Brien.'

He felt as much relief at her response as he would have after a long, tiring hunt for buffalo that ended in the finding of a big herd. 'All right then. Oh, I almost forgot. Smitty is selling me a little house he owns out on the Tulsa road, not far from the old fort. I can't tolerate sleeping here with all these other folks. That's part of our deal.'

Sarah beamed a wider smile on hearing that. 'That's wonderful. You'll be a property owner. I'd be happy to help you clean it up some.'

O'Brien nodded. 'Yes, ma'am. I mean, if it ain't a bother.

That would be just fine.'

At that moment Smith walked back into the office, looking quickly at Sarah to assess what had transpired in his absence. He was pleased to see her smiling more radiantly than he had ever seen her smile before. 'I see he told you.'

Sarah wiped at an eye unobtrusively. 'Yes. He told me.'

'Well, let's go, partner,' Smith boomed out. 'We got miles to cross if we want to make a start on that trip south. I put Reece in charge while we're gone. He's got a head on his shoulders.'

O'Brien rose, and Sarah did, too. 'We'll be looking for you when we get back,' he said quietly to her.

She took a deep breath. 'I'll be here,' she said. 'Probably at the town hall. I start my job for the mayor tomorrow.'

'You'll be the best thing that ever happened to this town,' Smith told her.

Outside on the street a few minutes later, after Smith had given Reece some last minute instructions, he and O'Brien mounted up and prepared to ride out. Sarah was watching from the doorway.

'We'll be gone at least a couple weeks,' Smith called down to her. 'Look in on Reece a couple times, Sarah, and see that he ain't scaring no passengers off.'

Sarah laughed lightly. Suddenly her world looked brighter to her than she could ever remember. 'I'll do that, Mr Smith.'

'Call me Smitty,' he told her.

O'Brien looked over at him. Smith had never let anybody call him Smitty except O'Brien.

Sarah nodded. 'All right. Smitty.'

'O'Brien and Sarah exchanged a smile then, and a moment later the two men were riding out of town with Sarah staring after them.

159

Without looking back, O'Brien knew she was still back there, watching them disappear off into the wilds of the Territory. Worrying over them already. Hoping they came back all right.

He hadn't felt that kind of concern for him since he left the Shenandoah.

He decided he liked it.